The Abyss line of cutting-edge psychological horror is committed to publishing the best, most innovative works of dark fiction available. ABYSS is horror unlike anything you've ever read before. It's not about haunted houses or evil children or ancient Indian burial grounds. We've all read those books, and we all know their plots by heart.

ABYSS is for the seeker of truth, no matter how disturbing or twisted it may be. It's about people, and the darkness we all carry within us. ABYSS is the new horror from the dark frontier. And in that place, where we come face-to-face with terror, what we find is ourselves.

"Thank you for introducing me to the remarkable line of novels currently being issued under Dell's Abyss imprint. I have given a great many blurbs over the last twelve years or so, but this one marks two firsts: first *unsolicited* blurb (*I* called *you*) and the first time I have blurbed a whole *line* of books. In terms of quality, production, and plain old story-telling reliability (that's the bottom line, isn't it?), Dell's new line is amazingly satisfying . . . a rare and wonderful bargain for readers. I hope to be looking into the Abyss for a long time to come."

—Stephen King

Please turn the page for more extraordinary acclaim . . .

HIGH PRAISE FOR
DENNIS ETCHISON

"America's premier writer of horror stories."
—Fantasy Newsletter

AND HIS PREVIOUS NOVEL ***SHADOWMAN***

"*Shadowman* demonstrates all of [Etchison's] strengths. . . . He tells an innately horrifying story that catches the reader off-balance at every step. *Shadowman* would be a subversive book in any context, but in the safe, imitative world of contemporary horror, it is a kind of terrorist raid." —Peter Straub

"THE BEST SHORT STORY WRITER IN THE FIELD TODAY, BAR NONE!" —Charles L. Grant

"Dennis Etchison is a tremendously accomplished writer . . . who both knows his cultural history and keenly surveys what popular culture's doing today."

—*Locus*

"BRILLIANT . . . HIGHLY ENTERTAINING . . . [SHADOWMAN IS] AN EXCELLENT BOOK . . . ETCHISON AT HIS BEST." —*The Grim Reader*

"[Shadowman is] filled with perfection and loss; always delicate, heartbreaking. Its language is brilliant, its images and moods dense with vision . . . a rich novel, gifted by thoughtful turns; haunting ease. It is upsetting and powerful."

—Richard Christian Matheson

"ONE HELL OF A FICTION WRITER."
—Stephen King

"Etchison is that rarest of genre writers . . . [his] nightmares and fears are intensely personal, and his genius is to make us realize that we share them."
—Karl Edward Wagner

"Etchison provides a very evocative sense of growing terror . . . [*Shadowman* is] one of those rare novels you're likely to read through in a single sitting, without even realizing how caught up you are."
—*Science Fiction Chronicle*

"One of the most innovative short story writers of the contemporary period . . . the most original living horror writer in America. In both subject matter and style, he has forged a contemporary horror milieu as new and daring as the film nightmares of David Cronenberg."
—*The Viking Encyclopedia of Horror and the Supernatural*

"THE STATE OF THE ART IN MODERN HORROR."
—*Publishers Weekly*

"*Shadowman* . . . reflects much of what makes Etchison great . . . unexpected twists, marvelously cinematic images and a disturbing resolution."—*Fangoria*

Also by Dennis Etchison

SHADOWMAN

METAHORROR

California Gothic

DENNIS ETCHISON

A DELL BOOK

Published by
Dell Publishing
a division of
Bantam Doubleday Dell Publishing Group, Inc.
1540 Broadway
New York, New York 10036

If you purchased this book without a cover you should be aware that this book is stolen property. It was reported as "unsold and destroyed" to the publisher and neither the author nor the publisher has received any payment for this "stripped book."

Copyright © 1995 by Dennis Etchison

The story outline for the motion picture *American Zombie* (pp. 55-72) was created in collaboration with Stephen Jones. Copyright © 1995 by Dennis Etchison and Stephen Jones.

Chapter Two of this novel was previously published in the anthology *Borderlands 4*, edited by Elizabeth E. Monteleone and Thomas F. Monteleone, under the title "A Wind from the South." Copyright © 1994 by Dennis Etchison.

All rights reserved. No part of this book may be reproduced or transmitted in any form or by any means, electronic or mechanical, including photocopying, recording, or by any information storage and retrieval system, without the written permission of the Publisher, except where permitted by law.

The trademark Dell® and Abyss® are registered in the U.S. Patent and Trademark Office.

ISBN: 0-440-21726-1

Printed in the United States of America

Published simultaneously in Canada

June 1995

10 9 8 7 6 5 4 3 2 1

OPM

To Kristina

It is a mistake to fancy that horror is associated inextricably with darkness, silence, and solitude. I found it in the glare of midafternoon . . .

—H. P. Lovecraft,
Cool Air

There was no wind in the valley.

The pines on the hills were so still they might have been painted there, etched on the horizon to separate the rim from the bowl of the sky. Farther down, morning dew clung to the live oaks and bands of mist hid the manzanita until the haze burned off. Then wild lilacs showed through, shades of gray turning purple and magenta and pale blue, and later the browns and greens of redwoods, as the sun rose higher and the forest came alive.

The distant fire trails remained two-dimensional, without perspective against the natural walls of the State Park. Only closer, in the canyons, was there some sense of depth, with rounded clumps of scrub and sage along the narrow access road. Here chips of quartz and granite glittered sharply in the unpaved dirt, ready to cut the tires of any Jeep or truck that passed this way.

But today it was the first of May, and time for another inspection.

The Forest Service usually made the rounds in pairs. A virulent strain of flu had temporarily reduced the force by nearly forty percent, so this morning there was only one man in the truck. He was thin with tight, sunburned lips, lank hair over a receding forehead and a shy, deferential face, just the sort of young man who might choose to work as far away as possible from cities and strangers and questions for which he had no ready answers. He carried his tools in back, shovels and saws and rope, chains and spare tires and a winch, with a first-aid kit and fire extinguisher in the cab, next to a geological survey map and the lunch he had packed in a Coleman chest, watched over by a shiny black Labrador retriever named Jimbo, who was his best friend.

It was the young man's job to keep the access road open, to check the terrain for erosion, and to note anything out of the ordinary. There were several privately-owned cabins on his route; he was instructed to see that they were secure, which meant a brief visual check and a notation in his logbook. Some of these were parcels under lifetime lease, old homesteads from long before the Department of the Interior had acquired the land. Others were subleased by the owners during the summer months, and in a few cases for year-round occupancy. The Forest Service did not care what went on in these cabins, so long as the brush was cut back and there was no sign of new construction without the proper permit. A wisp of wood smoke from a chimney, horses or mules or rows of cultivated vegetables were no one's business. Only a mud slide, a shack slipping off its bedrock foundation or obvious signs of burglary were reasons to stop. Otherwise he kept his distance and drove on by. He did not even carry a gun, and hardly ever had occasion to use the two-way radio in the truck. Once he had brought a tape player, but the music seemed out of place here, the mechanical rhythms of pop songs booming out incongruously over the panoramic landscape. No manufactured sounds could compete with such overpowering majesty. Respectful silence was part of the park's character, its dignity, here where the falling of a rock or the breaking of a branch or the rustling of a wing in the cathedral of a tree resounded for miles in every direction, the elements of an incomparable natural symphony.

So the gunshot startled him.

"Easy, boy," he said to his dog.

He lifted his foot from the accelerator. The echo decayed rapidly, pinpointing a location. It was close by, in the box canyon below. The short, high crack, followed immediately by a metallic clinking, meant that it was only someone target shooting, probably at a tin can. There was a cabin several hundred feet down the ravine, near the old stream.

More shots followed, with a slight pause between, the approximate length of time it takes to work the bolt on a single-action rifle. Each was accompanied by another clink.

"Sounds like a .22," he said, patting the dog. "Right, Jimbo?"

He idled the truck, waiting for the shooter to reload. A parchment lizard hesitated between his front tires, then scuttled away into the fir trees.

The dog put its paws on the dashboard.

"Easy," he said again.

The next shot was a roar.

This time it was definitely not a plinking rifle. It was a rapid-fire burst, the rounds so close together that they might almost have been a single explosion. The tone was lower, hard and deep; that meant larger caliber shells fired from a semiautomatic, the kind of weapon that is never certified for use on federal grounds. But hunting licenses were not under the jurisdiction of the Forest Service. A call to the Ranger Station would take care of the matter.

He picked up his radio microphone.

CALIFORNIA GOTHIC

There was a tiny thrashing in the needles under the fir tree as the lizard elevated itself, pumping up and down, one bulging eye sweeping the ravine.

Jimbo jumped out of the truck.

"Hey . . . !"

The dog pawed the earth where the lizard had been, then raised its head and concentrated on a point down the hillside.

He sighed, put down his microphone, climbed out and crossed the road. He tried to pet the dog but it was sleek and tense.

"What's wrong with you, boy? You've heard guns before . . ."

He followed Jimbo's glassy stare.

And saw something moving in the scrub below, a smear of flesh flickering through the branches of a pepper tree.

"It's only a skinny-dipper," he said, and lowered his eyes.

When he tried to hook his fingers under the choke chain the dog was already gone, scrambling over the edge.

A few seconds later he heard a yelp of pain.

"Jimbo?"

He hurried down, started running to keep ahead of himself and could not stop till he came to the trunk of an old madrone. He balanced there, brushing the red bark from his palms, and called again for the dog.

"Here, boy!"

Then he could not say anything else, because he saw her. She was kneeling at the bottom of the ravine, tending the dog. Jimbo sat on his haunches and offered his paw without resistance, as though humbling himself before a queen. Her body was slender with a muscled back, her shoulders and strong legs ruddy and her breasts and buttocks like white gold.

"He's okay," she called. "He picked up a piece of glass, is all."

She stood up, naked except for her straight, dark hair that was so long it might never have been cut.

"Thanks," he said, unable to look directly at her.

"Who are you?" There was no embarrassment, only curiosity in her voice.

"Sam," he managed to say.

"Hello, Sam."

She turned and walked back to the cabin.

He saw a wheelbarrow and a spade next to a large hole in the ground, and two saddle racks on the porch. The dog followed her to the porch and lay down by the barrel of a rifle, licking its paw.

"Sorry to bother you," he said, because it was necessary to say something. "I was just passing by. Come on, boy."

The dog did not move.

CALIFORNIA GOTHIC

He started across the yard.

"Watch out for the glass," she said.

He looked at his shoes and saw the shards underfoot. When he took a step they crunched, embedding in the soles of his boots. Most of the yard sparkled beneath a blanket of diamond dust, broken bottles that she had set up and shot down. There were also dozens, even hundreds of drilled, misshapen cans by the tree stumps. He made out a clean line worn into the dirt between the hill and the porch.

Miraculously, her bare feet were not scarred. They were perfect, flat and pink, without a mark on them. She had learned the route exactly.

At the porch she stopped with her back to him, her legs apart, braced. She bent down and took something from the shadows. When she finally turned around, she had an automatic pistol in one hand.

"I thought so," he said without flinching. "Colt .45, Army model. I heard it from up there, on the road."

She shucked the clip out of the handle, replaced it with a fresh one and worked the slide, chambering a round.

"You want to be careful," he told her. "The safety's off."

"I know."

She raised the gun. He tried to move aside. The muzzle followed, sweeping across his chest to a Michelob bottle propped up on the ground near his left foot. He froze as she fired once. The bottle exploded.

"Uh, nice shooting," he said, as the sound rolled away.

The big gun was steady in her hands. "Are you going to bust me?"

"Well, there's no law against target practice."

"Aren't you the fuzz?"

"Gee, I haven't heard that word in a long time." He made an effort to smile, took a deep breath and let it out slowly so that it puffed his cheeks. He tapped the patch on his short-sleeved shirt. "Don't worry. I'm only the Forest Service."

"Oh yeah," she said. "I've seen your truck."

"You have?"

"Right. Once a month. I forgot what day it was." She tilted her head quizzically, observing him. The gun was still in her hand but now it hung limply at the end of her wrist, its aim undecided. At last she lowered the hammer with her thumb. "Sam what?"

"Uh, Carlisle. What's *your* name?"

"Judy."

"Judy what?"

"Susie, I mean. Susan . . . Jones."

"Okay. Well, hi, Susie. You live here?"

She nodded.

"Not alone, though," he added.

CALIFORNIA GOTHIC

"Yes. Alone."

"I see." He nodded, too, as if he believed her. "This is the old Miller place, isn't it?"

"Miller?"

"The owner. So you must be subletting."

"Right," she said.

He kept nodding.

They stood that way, facing each other across the yard, the sun behind her, hiding the details of her features now that he was able to look at her. She made no move to cover herself, as though her nakedness were completely normal. There was a box of .22 longs next to the plinking rifle on the porch, below the saddles. The stirrup irons were corroded and had not been used in a long time.

"Where's your horse?" he asked.

"I had to put him down."

"Oh. That's tough."

"No, it wasn't. It was easy."

A few yards from the porch, the spade held fresh dirt. The earth around the hole was three or four feet high and the top of the mound was beginning to dry out like worm castings in the heat of the day.

"Is that why you're digging?"

"What?"

"A grave. For the horse."

"Right."

"That's hard work."

"I can handle it."

"What about the other one?"

"What other one?"

"You have two saddles."

"He died a long time ago."

She could not have been very old, not with a body so lithe and firm.

"You need a horse up here," he said. "If you don't have a truck. How do you get your supplies?"

"I've been to town, to the Safeway. But we brought a lot with us."

"We?"

"I mean I."

"How long ago was that?"

"Why?"

"I was just wondering," he said. "It must be pretty rough, cut off like this."

"I get by."

"I can see that."

A great tan hawk circled high in the currents overhead, closing in.

"Well, I'd better get going." He backed off carefully, staying on the footpath, as though retracing his way out of a minefield. "Come on, Jimbo."

But the dog was no longer on the porch.

"Where . . . ?"

Then, from inside the cabin, Jimbo began to bark.

CALIFORNIA GOTHIC

She turned swiftly and went in, holding the gun as if it were a flashlight.

When he got to the porch he heard a click. The sound was unmistakable: the hammer of the .45 cocking.

He looked around the door.

At first the cabin was black as night. Then the shadows sharpened and the edges of furniture showed. There were two straight-backed chairs, an old handmade table, empty kitchen shelves and a rug on the dusty wooden floor across the room, in front of a pot-bellied stove.

She was at another door in the far wall, holding the dog by the collar, the muzzle of the gun resting on top of the animal's skull.

"What's the matter?" he said.

She straightened up and the gun swung away, pointing at the floor. The dog scratched at the closed door. She used one perfect leg to push him back. The dog sniffed her skin, looked up at her eyes, and lay down at her feet.

"Nothing," she said.

"Here, Jimbo. It's late . . ."

"No, it's not."

"What time is it?" He could not read his Swiss Army watch. The cabin was dim, with very little light coming in from the windows. They were covered by a heavy, dark material, like blackout curtains. "I have to finish my rounds."

"Are you thirsty?"

"Well . . ." he said. She seemed to want him to stay. "Maybe a little."

She passed close to him on her way to the kitchen area. He looked away, and saw cardboard cartons on the floor, under the bare shelves. Everything in the house including the clock must have been packed away, except for the table and chairs and the rug by the wood-burning stove. If he had wandered in on his own, he could not have been sure that anyone lived here.

He glanced down at the nearest carton. The top was open. In the stray light from the front door he saw that it contained old magazines from the sixties and seventies, *Eye* and *Other Scenes* and *Mother Jones* mostly, and some folded copies of newspapers like *The Berkeley Barb*, *The East Village Other*, *The Avatar* and *Homefires*. When he flipped through them bits of cut paper fluttered out. There was also a file folder bulging with handwritten letters and, sticking out of the top, a photograph of her standing next to a young man with sideburns and long hair; a few books, *You Are All Sanpaku* and *The Anarchist's Cookbook* and *Public Works;* and even bottles of homeopathic medicine wrapped in a T-shirt. It was an old Grateful Dead shirt, with the LIVE FROM THE MARS HOTEL emblem silkscreened in reverse on the back.

CALIFORNIA GOTHIC

"See anything you like?" she said.

She bent over and took two tin cups out of another carton. She set these on the sink and poured water from a one-gallon plastic bottle.

"This is a collector's item," he said, holding up the shirt. "My dad used to have one."

"Take it," she said. "Here." She handed him a cup.

"Thanks," he said, drinking deeply. "This is good water."

"The stream. From the top of the mountains. No toxic pollution."

She took her cup and went over to the rug in front of the stove and sat down cross-legged.

He repositioned one of the chairs and lowered himself onto it.

"So," he said. "I guess you don't get much company up here."

"Are you going to tell anyone?"

"You mean the .45? Don't worry about it."

"I mean about me." She watched his eyes.

"No reason to," he said. "Do you practice a lot?"

"I have to."

"Yeah, I guess you do. Timber wolves, bear . . ."

"They don't bother me."

She lay back on the rug.

"It looks like you're moving out," he said, averting his eyes.

"As soon as I get rid of everything."

"Do you have a mule?"

"Not anymore."

"You could use a truck."

"That's what I was thinking."

"You can rent one in town. But it's a long way down."

"I know."

"Maybe I could give you a lift. We could even bring a few boxes."

"I don't need them. I'm going home. To a real house."

"Yeah? Whereabouts?"

"L.A."

"You have friends there?"

"My old man."

"Oh." He emptied his cup and set it on the floor. "Well, thanks for the drink."

"I haven't seen him in a long time."

The young man was silent for a moment. Then he said, "If you still need that ride, I could come back by. After I finish."

"Do they know where you are?"

"Not exactly."

She studied him from one elbow, raising her knee slightly. "Then you could be anywhere. Or nowhere."

"You could say that."

Her knee moved as her legs opened and closed and opened.

CALIFORNIA GOTHIC

"Maybe you better put this on," he said, and tossed her the shirt.

"I don't want it. I have everything I need in my pack." She extended one long arm, indicating a hiker's backpack next to the stove.

"What are you going to do with the boxes?"

"Bury them."

"Why?"

"So nobody will know I was here. Except you."

"Doesn't anybody ever come?"

"Only the campers. Sometimes they stay by the river, and I get their cans and bottles."

"How old are you?" he said.

"How old do I look?"

"You look eighteen. But I can't tell from here."

She lay back the rest of the way on the animal skin rug and dangled the shirt like a white flag. "That's because you're too far away."

He got up slowly. He went over and took the shirt from her. Then he dropped down to his knees.

"Take your shoes off first," she said.

"Are you sure you're eighteen?"

She sat up and untied one of his shoelaces.

As she did this, he reached for the backpack as though embarrassed, unzipped it. There were jeans inside, sandals, a madras shift, some packets of freeze-dried food and a survival knife with a compass on the end and a hollow com-

15

partment in the handle to hold matches. He stuffed the shirt in on top of the knife and closed the zipper.

"There," he said. "So you don't get cold in L.A."

"It's always warm there. That's what they say." She was fiddling with the other shoelace, trying to get both boots off.

He looked down at her. "What about your husband?"

"I don't even know what he looks like anymore."

She lay back and spread her arms.

"How long has it been?"

"Ten years. Twelve. At least."

"That's not possible," he said. "You were only a kid then."

"Maybe I'm older. Maybe I didn't change."

He ran his hand haltingly over her breasts and down to her belly and her legs. "Maybe," he said. "If you say so."

The dog whined from its place in front of the closed door.

"What's that?" he asked.

"The bedroom."

"Want to go in there?"

"No."

"Why not?"

She pulled free of his hand and sat up.

"What's wrong?"

CALIFORNIA GOTHIC

She did not answer.

"Okay," he said. "I gotta go, anyway."

"Yes, you do." She stood and walked to the kitchen.

The dog reared its head, sniffed, and pawed at the door again.

"What's the smell?" he said.

"Don't open the door."

"Why?"

He got up and went over to Jimbo and pushed on the latch before she could get there to stop him. The door swung open.

"I warned you," she said.

"Oh, Jesus, *what is that?* Who—?"

The dog growled.

He held Jimbo back and slammed the door shut and covered his mouth.

When he turned around she was no longer there.

The backpack was gone, and the gun was not in the kitchen where she had left it.

He ran to the front door. He saw the hole she had dug outside, deep enough for the contents of the cabin so that nothing important would be left behind. And now he saw the five-gallon can of gasoline so that everything that was not covered over could be torched. There was the path through the broken bottles to the road above and his truck with the two-way radio. But he did not have his shoes. He was about to go back for them when the long knife came around from behind the door where she had been waiting and cut his windpipe. The dog barked and leaped, only to drop out of the air with a whimper when the gun went off.

By the time the firefighters got there, she was miles away.

Chapter One

There was a breeze in the backyard.

Markham brushed the dirt from his eyelids and raised his head above the mounded earth. The sun glared over the roof, casting hard shadows under the spider legs of the swing, bleaching the grass, withering the leaves of the stunted palm trees and the aloe plants that were turning a sickly, dehydrated yellow-white nearer the house, the color of jaundice and neglect. And yet the air moved against his face, momentarily cool, as if his skin were dripping with aftershave instead of sweat. He stood on his shovel and smiled. It was a relief to know that there were still signs of life aboveground, where some things had not yet been buried.

Across the yard, the screen door clattered open.

Eddie came out of the kitchen, carrying what

appeared to be a small, dark coffin. The boy hesitated on the back porch, eyes down. Then he started slowly for the garage.

"Hi," Markham called to him.

The boy looked around.

"Oh hi, Dad."

Markham stepped up onto the blade of the shovel with both feet, so that the rest of his face showed above the dry grass.

"What's that?"

"Stuff." The boy kept walking. It was not a coffin, after all, but one of those long, flat, wood-grained cardboard boxes made for storing things under beds. As he walked, a magazine worked its way out of the box and flapped to the ground. It was a copy of *Shock Zone*. There was a flash of red: a full-page photo of a face running with gore, piercing, bloodshot eyes peering from deep within decomposing flesh. "Mom said to put it outside."

"She did?" Markham turned his head to follow the boy, a gopher's-eye view. "How come?"

"Till you get my room painted."

That means she's getting impatient, thought Markham. She's taking the law into her own hands.

The boy set the box down on the grass, retrieved the copy of *Shock Zone* and lifted the lid. He flipped carefully through the rest of his magazines to make sure they were all there.

CALIFORNIA GOTHIC

"Well," said Markham, "put it on the shelf under the tarp, I guess. For now. Do you need a hand?"

"No."

"Sure?"

"Yeah."

The thirteen-year-old got another hold on the box and carried it the rest of the way across the yard.

He's pissed off, Markham thought. I can't blame him. He doesn't like changes. How's he going to handle it when we move? Not any better than I will, probably. God help him.

An orange streak left the porch and trailed the boy to the garage like an afterimage, a trick of the morning light. Markham's field of vision blurred as perspiration ran into his eyes. He wiped his forehead on his sleeve.

The view cleared and he saw the kitten darting after Eddie, tracking him suspiciously. The cat did not like changes, either. How would they move him? In a box? He would be older in a few months, but not old enough to understand.

The kitten sidestepped a cluster of dandelions, crouched down and pounced, arching its back and batting wildly. The flowers that had already gone to seed now exploded, releasing white puffballs. Markham watched them settle over the dying foliage, adhering to the curled funnels of bromeliads, the desiccated swords of aloes, the drooping, inverted triangles of ivy. The kitten pursued one of the spores through the garden to the edge of the hole Markham had dug.

Enjoy it while you can, he thought. Wherever we move, there won't be another backyard like this one.

The dandelion spore alighted on a mount of dirt. Within the clods a drying earthworm secreted protective moisture and cranked its segments in a desperate circle, signaling for help. Markham gently plucked the worm out between thumb and forefinger and dropped it into the darkness at his feet. Then he caught the spore and held it close to his face. It vibrated like a one-celled sea creature under a microscope, pulsing in the tide of his heartbeat, before breaking apart on the breeze. He balanced there, his head in sunlight and his body planted in the earth, and stared at his empty fingers.

From the next yard came the whir of an air conditioner. A few blocks away, the Saturday playgroup at the elementary school laughed and bounced hollow rubber balls on blacktop. A car downshifted and inched along the street in front of the house. He heard birds talking in the trees and a cloud of insects humming, while in the garage his son unfolded a stepladder. Somewhere a dog barked. The kitten made no sound. It lay on one side, only inches from him, and

CALIFORNIA GOTHIC

wrapped its tiny translucent claws around his thumb, then tensed as across the yard the screen door creaked open again.

"Dan?"

"Over here," he said, focusing past his thumb.

Evie held the door back with one shoulder, an unwieldy stack of file folders in her arms. She had on a pale pink tank top and white shorts and her hair was tied in a loose ponytail, with a single long strand left to bob over her forehead. She used her knee to shift the weight of the stack so that she could get a better grip.

"What are you doing?" she said.

"Digging," he said. "Need some help?"

"No, thanks. Do you want these?"

"What are they?"

"Old income tax records. Why are we saving them?"

"We're supposed to."

"For how long?"

He had to think about it. "Seven years. That's the statute of limitations."

"Who told you that?"

"Our accountant."

"Did he say seven, or three?"

"Call him and find out."

Evie blew the strand of hair away from her eyes. "It doesn't matter. Either way, we're safe now."

She went to the trash can, got the lid off and

dumped the files. They shuffled down in yellowed layers. She put the lid back on and faced him.

"How about some lunch?"

"Not yet," he said.

"What are you digging?"

"Come here and I'll show you."

She walked carefully with her bare feet, avoiding the clumped dirt. When she came to the edge she bent over to pick up the kitten, and Markham glimpsed her breasts through the scoop neck of the tank top. Her skin was glistening.

He thought, She could pass for twenty-four. Does she know that? Probably not. If I tried to tell her, she wouldn't believe me.

She held the kitten close to her cheek, as though it were a baby rose, and kissed it.

"What do you want to show us?"

He lowered his head below ground again. The hole was almost too narrow for him to turn around. Now, away from the sun, he was blind for a few seconds and the sounds of the neighborhood faded away. He felt his knuckles brush the crumbling strata, then a smooth, rounded curve of glass. He pulled it free and stood, holding the treasure high.

"What's that?"

"An original Royal Crown Cola bottle," he said proudly. It was ancient but unbroken, with the yellow-and-red pyramid logo still intact on one side. "Twelve ounces. They don't make them anymore."

"Really?" she said, unimpressed.

From another layer near the surface he liberated a flattened Pet Milk can, a Yoo-Hoo bottle, an aluminum TV dinner tray, an encrusted cap pistol that was missing half of its imitation pearl handle. As he stood up again, the sounds of the morning returned.

"Look at all this, will you?"

"Very nice," she said. "Just what we need. More junk."

"These are collector's items, Evie. I used to have a gun like this when I was ten . . ."

"It's junk."

She was right, of course, but he would not give up. "I wish you could see down here. It must go back forty years."

"Was this a landfill?"

"No, just somebody's backyard. You know how it is. Things get dropped, lost, but they don't go away. Like fossils. It's a record of the people who lived here before us, the things that mattered to them."

"Did you find my emerald ring?"

He remembered. It had flown off her hand one day while they were landscaping the backyard, shortly after they moved here. Sometimes she still tossed and turned next to him and spoke of the ring in her dreams, filled with anxiety and remorse. It had been her mother's.

"I'm looking."

A blue jay squawked from a treetop. The kitten's ears pointed like miniature radar dishes, zeroing in on the sound. The sparrows fell silent. The kitten opened its eyes wide and swatted at a curious bee, as a cloud of gnats scattered and moved on, re-forming near the oldest palm tree. The blue jay squawked another warning and the kitten's hackles rose, the red hairs standing up on its back as Evie tried to hold it. Worn brakes screaked in the street. A buzzer rang jarringly in the schoolyard and the children stopped laughing. Playtime was over.

Evie flexed her knees and squatted down, holding the kitten protectively.

"You're not digging a new fishpond, are you?"

"I'm fixing the pipes."

"What pipes?"

"The ones to the sprinkler system."

"Why bother?" she asked sincerely.

"It'll make the house easier to sell. We can't show it with the yard like this."

She looked past him at the rambling roses and the ferns and the trees he had planted, now strung with drying vines and shrunken runners of ivy, the redwood lattices that were faded and warped, the lava rock waterfall that had once sparkled in the sunlight and sung to them. It

CALIFORNIA GOTHIC

was meant to be a tropical paradise right here in their backyard, something to set their tract house lot apart from so much suburban blight. And so it might have been, if the underground pipes had not broken last year. For a while the rains had brought it alive again; then the drought returned. With the store to take up so much of their time, neither of them remembered to water it regularly. The drip soaker lay flat as a deflated snakeskin among the weeds. He looked with her, and saw his folly.

In the street, the worn brakes sounded again, coming this way.

The kitten jumped out of her hands and ran for cover.

"It's your day off," she said. Her knees were white as knuckles as she studied him at close range.

"I know. But it has to be done, and we can't afford to hire anybody . . ."

A faint smile twitched at the sides of her mouth. She moistened her lips.

"Dan . . ."

"Don't worry. I'll start on Eddie's room later. I need a new brush. And rollers."

She leaned closer, her eyes at half-mast. "Danny . . ."

"I was thinking. I may as well paint the kitchen, too. I'll buy some dropcloths at Builder's Bonanza, as soon as I finish here. Tomorrow's Sunday, so if I can get one coat on both rooms—"

"Danny," she whispered, "will you shut up?"

She braced her elbow on the ground and turned her face sideways, her cheek almost touching the dirt. Then she kissed him. As she pulled away, a silver strand connected her lips to his, like a fragment of spiderwebbing.

"What was that for?"

"Because."

"Why?"

"Because you're special," she said, watching his mouth.

He let go of his spade and reached for her.

Eddie came out of the garage.

The brakes squealed, directly in front of their house now.

"There's the mail truck," she said, rising. "I'd better go see."

"Tell him to fix his brakes, while you're at it."

She went inside.

"What's that?" said Eddie. He moved the dirty cap gun with the toe of his Nike.

"That," said Markham, "is a Fanner Fifty."

"What's a Fanner Fifty?" said Eddie, as if testing his father to see if he knew his own name and what day of the week it was, and what year.

"It's the same gun I had when I was your age."

"The *same* gun?"

"Well, the same kind."

CALIFORNIA GOTHIC

"When you were *my* age?"

"A little younger, maybe. See the hammer, the way it's flattened out? That's so you could shoot off a whole role of caps, fifty shots, at one time."

"Great, Dad," said Eddie, vaguely embarrassed. He was eager to change the subject. "I put the *Shock Zone*s on the shelf. Is it going to rain?"

"I don't think so. Why?"

"The tarp's got holes in it. Just like the roof. What if it rains and all my magazines get wrecked?"

"It won't. I have to get some new tarps, anyway, before I paint your room."

Eddie groaned. "When are you doing *that?*"

"This afternoon, maybe. Want to go to Builder's Bonanza?"

"No, thanks." Eddie sounded as though he would as soon kiss his grandmother in her casket. "I have to meet Tommy."

"Did you tell Mom?"

"Yeah."

"Will you be home for dinner?"

"I don't know. We're going to the mall."

"Need a ride?"

"His brother's dropping us."

"The Cineplex?"

"Yeah."

"What's playing?"

"*American Zombie II.*"

31

Markham winced. "Sounds good."

"Tommy's brother says it's not as good as Part One. But he's a jock." Eddie warmed to the subject, kneeling down next to the hole. "Stefan J. says it's better."

"Stefan?"

"The editor of *Shock Zone*."

"Oh."

"It's in Dolby-Carver."

"You mean stereo?"

"Sonic Holography," the boy explained. "The sound comes from all around, in back of you, even over your head. In Part One, when Justin Travis—that's the American Zombie—when he's up on top of the roller coaster at the end, you can hear the bullets go by!"

He loves it, thought Markham. And he knows what he's talking about. He ought to go to film school, maybe UCLA or Cal Arts. I'd like to see the movies he makes.

"When's Part Three coming out?" he asked.

"Next year, probably."

"Maybe we can see that one together." Like we used to, thought Markham, remembering the John Carpenter retrospective last year. Or was it two years ago? Evie wouldn't go, of course. But I would.

"Okay," said Eddie, "I guess."

The back door opened.

"There you are," said Evie.

CALIFORNIA GOTHIC

"Hi, Mom," Eddie said, hurrying past her into the house.

"I was looking for you . . ."

" 'Bye, Mom."

"Where's he off to?" said Evie, crossing the yard.

"Tommy's," said Markham. "You know, over on Bradfield?"

"Hm. I have to meet Jean in a few minutes. Doesn't he want me to drive him?"

"Not anymore," he told her.

"Well," she said, "they're nice people. Did he ask you for money?"

"No."

"Good. He already got ten from me. An advance on his column." She sighed and remembered that she was holding a packet of envelopes. "Here's the mail."

"Anything good?"

"Citibank, Discover, American Express . . ."

"Besides bills."

"Let's see. Lloyd Curry's new catalogue, one from Robert Gavora, Dreamhaven Books . . . And here's a letter for you."

"Who's it from?"

"There's no return address. Maybe it's from your girlfriend."

"Does it smell like perfume?"

She sniffed it. "Afraid not."

"Then does it smell like money?"

"I'm not sure. It's been so long."

"Open it."

As she tore off the end of the envelope, the phone rang in the kitchen.

"Oh God," she said, "that's Jean. What time is it? Here." She dropped the envelopes and ran for the back door.

The catalogues and bills plopped down, knocking some of the dirt back into the hole. He picked out the envelope and finished opening it. The sun was higher now and the piled-up earth was baking in grainy clumps. A rivulet of sand poured over the edge, burying his shoes.

The envelope contained a single sheet of typing paper folded into thirds. It seemed to be stuck together. As the sun's rays fell on the paper, he saw that something was glued to the other side of the mottled surface.

It was a collage, made from pictures cut out of an old magazine and pasted to the white bond. The pictures were taken from a seventies fashion layout, featuring several different models in trendy clothes. Some pieces were missing, but those that were left had been rearranged to form a jigsaw. The pieces did not quite connect. He thought of the dismembered limbs of a paper doll. Mismatched lettering had been pasted at the top of the page:

CALIFORNIA GOTHIC

> Dear Danny—
> I'm coming home.
> Wait for me!
> Love,
> Jude

The paper began to shake in his hands as a warmer breeze entered the yard. He leaned back against the dirt and read it again in the beam of light that now angled down into the hole he had dug for himself, revealing every detail of mulch, soil, gravel and dank clay, and the stratified edges of the forgotten debris that had been buried there for so long.

Chapter
Two

As Evie ran through the house, the morning light followed her. There was a white burst in each window, as if her passing had triggered a row of flashbulbs outside. Near the bedroom, she thought she saw a tall, dark outline squeeze from one pane to the next, pacing her, but the glass was so old that it flowed with distortion and she was unsure whether anyone was really there. It was not until she had peeled off her top and shorts and was about to step into the shower that the doorbell rang.

"Eddie, could you . . . ?"

But of course he couldn't. Her son had already gone, on his way to meet his friends and then to the mall.

"Dan?" she called, hoping that her husband would hear.

She stood with one hand on the hot water faucet and the other on the edge of the shower curtain, and waited. But Dan was still in the backyard. Too far away.

The bell rang again.

She reached for her robe. It was not on the back of the door. That's right, she thought, I put it in the laundry basket to be washed.

There was no time to get dressed. Should she ignore the bell? No, it might be United Parcel with a shipment intended for the store; then she or Dan would have to make a special trip just to pick it up.

She found his terrycloth robe in a heap at the end of the bed, where he had left it.

"Coming!" she shouted, tying the robe closed, and padded through to the living room.

She went first to the front window and peeked around the curtain. She could see only half of the porch, but it appeared to be empty, except for a long shadow cast by the overhang. Then something skittered across the lawn. She turned her head quickly, following a small pile of leaves that blew past on the sidewalk. Farther down the street, the mail truck rounded the corner, and a compact car idled under the stop sign. The car looked familiar. Was it Dan's? That meant he had already left, without saying good-bye.

She let the curtain fall and opened the door. "Yes?"

A young woman stood there in profile, as

though about to give up and move on. Beyond her, the lawn crackled with oak leaves. A wind had come up, as if from nowhere.

"I'm sorry to bother you," she said uncertainly, "but . . ."

Evie had never seen her before. At least there was no sample case in her hand; with any luck, she was not selling anything. That was a relief.

"It's all right," said Evie, relaxing slightly. "What can I—?"

"Well, you see . . ." She was hardly more than a girl, in her late teens or early twenties at most, though with the noonday sunlight behind her it was hard to be sure. Her hair was short and plain and she wore a loose, knee-length cotton dress several sizes too large, and no belt, as if to conceal her figure. "What street is this?" she asked finally.

"Stewart Way."

"Oh. I was afraid I took a wrong turn."

Did that mean she had, or hadn't?

"What address are you looking for?"

She had no reason to hide her body. From what Evie could see of her, long wiry arms, no stomach and short-toed pink feet, she was a perfect size four.

"I don't know. The school."

"Greenworth Elementary?" Was she walking? Barefoot? "You're almost there. Take a left at the corner, and then another left. You can't miss it."

"Thanks."

She made no move to leave, but lingered as though she had not yet said what was on her mind. Was she really going to the school? Maybe even a size two, thought Evie. I used to be that thin, once.

"Is there anything else?" Where was her watch? She had taken it off in the bathroom. "Because I'm kind of late. I was supposed to meet someone at twelve-thirty. For lunch." She gave the younger woman—girl?—a friendly but dismissive smile and started to shut the door.

"Is it far?"

"Just around the corner."

"I mean, where you're having lunch."

"What?" Evie wondered what business it was of hers. "Not really. Just over the hill."

"That's good." The girl looked at her wristwatch. "It's only eleven-fifteen."

"Is that all?" said Evie, surprised. "I thought it was twelve, at least."

The girl continued to stand there, the yellow-white light behind her, as the oak trees across the street shook down more leaves. Evie heard a scrabbling on the roof, twigs or tiny claws. The kitten? She felt a rush of radiant heat from the porch, moving the hair over her forehead, brushing the nap of her robe. Dan's robe. She retied it more securely.

"Do you think . . . ?"

CALIFORNIA GOTHIC

"What?" asked Evie.

"Could I please have a drink of water? The wind, it's so hot . . ."

"It's a Santa Ana."

"A what?"

"It always comes this time of year."

"Why?"

She was not from around here. "I'm not sure. But it's a warm wind from the south—Mexico, I think. Below the border, anyway." As the trees rustled and waved, Evie opened the door wider. "You don't have to stand out there. Come in."

As she closed the door, the whispering chorus of leaves was silenced. Evie felt better; it had made her uneasy. Then she heard a ceiling beam creak, hammering into place over them. There was a faint scurrying from the fireplace as the wind rearranged the ashes in the grating. It had found a way to get into the house. She would have to tell Dan to close the flue.

"I'll get your water."

She started for the kitchen, then glanced back. The girl was standing awkwardly by the sofa. Was she looking for a place to sit? Evie paused to remove the morning newspaper from the cushions.

"My name's Eve, by the way. Eve Markham."

"I know."

She was dark, probably Hispanic, Evie noticed. Or was it only a deep tan? "How?"

"From the mailbox."

The odd moment passed as easily as a skipped heartbeat. She expected the girl to offer her own name in return. She waited.

"Oh," Evie said after a few seconds. "Well, hi."

"Hi."

She went to the kitchen, took down one of the tall glasses, filled it quickly and returned.

"I didn't ask if you wanted ice."

"What? Oh, no. This is fine." The girl took a sip, that was all, and set the glass on the table in front of her.

She was seated comfortably on the sofa and the hastily-piled newspapers were nowhere to be seen. Had she moved them? Where? Evie wondered if she might be a housekeeper, looking for a job. But that made no sense. Why this house? Evie put it out of her mind.

"Do you live in the neighborhood?" Evie asked, sitting down in the easy chair.

"I'll be moving in soon. As soon as I find the right place."

Evie heard a car pass through the intersection at the corner, going away. She lowered her eyes while she tried to think of something else to say, and saw her knees poking out under the robe, as though it were not Dan's but her own short one instead. She covered her legs, and noted the veins on the backs of her hands. They made her look older, middle-aged. She was aware of the

CALIFORNIA GOTHIC

blood pulsing in her wrists, which were glistening. She touched her face, her neck. Her skin felt hot. It must have been the wind. Now she needed that shower more than ever. Why was there no clock in the living room?

"You have a child at the elementary school?" she asked.

"Not yet. I wanted to see the other children first. Is that when they have their lunch, at noon?"

It had been so long—a year? no, more—since her own son had gone there that Evie could hardly remember. The school was close enough that Eddie had come home for lunch most days, even when she and Dan were at work.

"I think so. But there aren't any classes today, only the playgroup."

The girl took another small sip of her water. Was there something wrong with it? Sorry I don't have bottled, Evie thought.

"You'll have to excuse me," she said, "but I really should—"

There was a wrenching sound from the backyard, and something fell with a terrible crash.

She hurried through the long house to the back porch.

The yard looked different somehow; at first she could not be sure why. For one thing, there was more sky showing than there should have been. Then she realized that one of the trees

Dan had planted between the house and the garage had fallen over. No, not fallen but broken, the top half lying in a pile of dry, misshapen branches and withered, unborn fruit, near the two dwarf palms. The trunk was split sharply and the bark stripped back to expose the soft white center, like a ragged piece of chicken meat that has been peeled away from the bone.

The girl was right behind her.

"The tree," said Evie. "I can't believe it. At least it didn't hit the house."

"Was it the wind?"

"Yes, I suppose so." What else?

"I'm sorry."

"That's all right. It's not your fault! He should have watered it more."

"Who?"

"Dan. My husband."

"I didn't see his name on the mailbox."

It was there. *Dan & Eve Markham.* She remembered the day he placed the adhesive letters on the box at the curb. He had done that, hadn't he? Unless they had peeled off.

She considered the broken tree, and felt a pang of sadness. They had neglected the backyard for so long. Once there had been a garden, lush and vibrant. How many years ago? With all the dead plants, and now this, it looked more like a cemetery overrun with weeds. But there was nothing to do about it now.

"Dan won't be very happy, when he gets home."

"What does your husband do?" asked the girl, as they walked back to the living room.

"He has a bookstore—we do. New and used. Minor Arcana, on Main and Second."

"Is that where he is now?"

"I hope not. This is his day off." Mine, too, she thought. At least it was supposed to be.

Still, it was good that she was not alone. If she had not answered the doorbell, she would have been in the shower when it happened. She imagined herself running through the house at the sound of the crash, dripping water . . .

"I'm glad you were here," Evie said.

"So am I."

"Do you want more water?"

"He must be very smart, your husband."

Evie laughed, releasing the tension. "He's the most intelligent man I ever met. That's why I married him. Or one of the reasons."

"Did he get his degree?"

"Well, not quite. He spent years at college, but he never graduated. He only took the classes he liked." It seemed a peculiar question. "What about your husband?"

"He has his own business. And he's very smart, too. We're going to have a nice house, with lots of windows, just like this one. As soon as we get settled."

Evie leaned back in the chair and took a better look at the younger woman. Actually she might not have been so young, after all; it was hard to tell. Her hair was unstylish, as if she had cut it herself and was now waiting to see how it would grow out. The windows were behind the sofa so that her features were backlighted, neutral, but Evie was sure that she wore no makeup. Her legs were strong and well-shaped, with small ankles. And there was the wristwatch, a man's Swiss Army model, on her left arm. But no ring.

She met dozens of people every day, many absolute strangers who came into the store in search of a book. Some of them did not know the name of the author or the title, or even what exactly they were looking for. Evie knew how to talk to them, to put them at their ease and make them feel comfortable, to draw them out and learn what they were really after. Sometimes they did not want anything but conversation. In that case she still tried to satisfy them before sending them on their way, so they would come back. Now, however, she was not in the shop, and this was not a customer. What the young woman wanted was unclear. Evie felt at a disadvantage. This one knew the power of silence. It was a way of maintaining the upper hand. But for what purpose?

"So you have children of your own?" Of

CALIFORNIA GOTHIC

course she does, Evie thought. She hadn't said so, not exactly, but why else would she be interested in the school?

"Do you?"

"One son," said Evie. "His name's Edward. He just turned thirteen."

She decided to leave it at that. Her natural impulse would have been to tell the woman all about Eddie, as much as she could stand to hear, his brilliance and precocity. But now for some reason she felt instinctively protective. She was relieved that he was not here.

"Is he at school?"

"Not today. It's Saturday. Remember?"

"Then where?"

Evie was conscious of a chill in the air. She fingered the edge of the robe, pulling it closed at her throat.

"With a friend." Yes, the Oshidari boy, over on Bradfield. That was right, wasn't it?

"Is your husband coming back?"

"Of course he is. Why wouldn't he?"

"I'd like to . . . meet him."

Evie stood. "Excuse me. I have to get ready now."

"Are you sure?"

What did *that* mean? "I'm afraid so. It's late."

"Is it?"

Danny, she thought, where are you? "What does that watch of yours say?"

49

The woman looked at her wrist. She tapped the crystal. "It stopped."

"When?"

"I don't know."

Evie went to the bedroom doorway and peered in at the clock on the nightstand.

"It's twelve-thirty!" she said.

"You should have a watch."

"I do," Evie snapped. "I took it off for my shower, and then you rang the bell."

"You need a clock in the living room. I'm going to have one, in my new house."

Evie pulled the front door wide. "I'm sure you will," she said. "Good-bye."

In the bedroom, she glanced around for some sign of her husband's clothes, even his socks by the bed, but they were not there. They were with the laundry, waiting to be washed. Weren't they? She had the urge to go to the back porch, where the washer and dryer were, just to be sure. There was no time. But if she did, she could look in at her son's room on the way. Why? To see that his clothes, his possessions were still there? She scanned the empty bedroom, frantic. Where were her son's childhood drawings? She had taped them to the wall years ago, hadn't she? *Hadn't she?*

She felt fear then, rising up through her body, going for her throat. Her hands clenched into fists, her fingers so small, her knuckles white as bones ready to pop through the skin. Where was her ring? Had she taken it off in the bathroom?

She struggled to form a name on her lips. Dan, she thought. That was it. And the name of her son. Edward.

Where were they?

A warm wind filled the room, flushing her cheeks.

The front door, she realized. She had left it open.

She went back to the living room.

There was the woman, in the doorway. She was standing in profile again, the hot wind blowing past her into the house, catching her dress so that it billowed out from her body. Now, the dress inflated with air, she appeared to be much heavier, by twenty or thirty pounds at least. The heat blurred, creating a mirage between Evie and the door, so that the woman's legs seemed suddenly thick, grown strong enough to carry the added weight, her ankles swollen and bloated.

"What do you want from me?" Evie said, reeling.

The hot wind subsided, moving on, and something left the house. The woman's dress deflated, hanging once more in loose folds. But, as Evie watched, she saw with perfect clarity that the woman was no longer slender. The front of the dress remained distended like a balloon, straining to cover a round, unmistakably swollen belly, where before it had been absolutely flat and empty.

"Nothing," said the other woman, and twisted the gold ring on her left hand. Then she turned to leave at last, smiling as if she had a secret, something too new and too personal, too private to share with anyone, least of all a stranger, just yet.

Chapter Three

Justin Travis is a young research scientist at the Olympia Chemical Company.

One night, working after hours, he discovers a mistake in the computer readout. He runs the figures again, but there's no doubt about it:

Something is dangerously wrong.

He must get to his boss, the CEO of Olympia Chemical, before it's too late.

On the way, he calls his girlfriend on his cellular phone.

Stacey, a secretary, works the mainframe computer at Olympia. She's home now—waiting for him.

"Where are you, Justin?"

"Sorry. I got hung up. There was something about the figures—"

"The food's cold!"

"I'll make it up to you."

"Just don't make dates that you can't keep."

"This is the last time, promise. I had to be sure. . . . See you later?"

"Justin, we have to talk. But not now. It's late."

She breaks the connection.

He forgot that she made dinner for him. But the numbers are important. He bites into a chili dog from a fast-food stand, and drives on . . .

To a construction site in the San Fernando Valley, where Olympia Chemical is co-developing a new housing tract.

In the office trailer, his boss, Robert Marston, is going over the blueprints with Ben, the Construction Manager, as Justin enters.

"Mr. Marston, I have something to show you."

"Can't it wait?"

"No, sir, it can't."

Justin hands Marston a printout.

"PCB, lead, radon levels all okay . . . Everything seems to be in order."

"Now look at the latest soil analysis."

CALIFORNIA GOTHIC

"But I took the first sample myself," says Marston.

"Exactly."

According to the new figures, the ground they're building on is unsafe.

"That means there will be cancer," Justin tells him, "birth defects, mutation, genetic bonding with organic material . . . We've got to stop construction!"

Marston can't believe it. His company has made a fortune with a patented decontamination process that renders any land —even a toxic-waste dump—safe for human habitation.

"Not this time," says Justin. "We made a mistake. The trucks were loaded with the wrong mix. Instead of neutralizing the area, we sprayed *more poison* into the ground!"

Marston signals for the Construction Manager to leave.

"Who else knows about this?" he asks Justin, shaken.

"No one—yet."

"Go home, Justin. I'll take care of everything."

"I'm glad I got to you in time, sir."

"So am I."

* * *

As Justin leaves the site, another car paces him . . .

Trying to force him off the road.

Justin swerves—but too late.

Ahead are the Olympia tanker trucks, loaded with the deadly chemicals.

He crashes into a truck, and the chemicals pour down over his car!

He climbs out of the wreck, contaminated, and staggers a few feet before collapsing . . .

As his car melts in a yellow-green cloud of toxic fumes.

At the hospital, Justin is pronounced dead on arrival.

Marston confers with Dr. Winter, the Chief of Surgery.

"I don't want this to get out," Marston tells him.

"Why the secrecy, Bob?"

"There was a spill. If the newspapers get wind of it, that could mean some nasty publicity."

"It's against hospital policy . . ."

"Remember the Children's Wing, Doug. I wouldn't want to withdraw the endowment."

* * *

CALIFORNIA GOTHIC

Later, an orderly wheels Justin's body to the subbasement.

In the morgue room, the orderly can't resist a peek under the sheet.

Justin's corpse is blistered with chemical burns. And there is a lumpy brown paste on his mouth—the chili dog he ate shortly before he died.

"What *is* that shit?" mutters the orderly. "You should watch it, man. You are what you eat. Pork will kill you . . ."

But Justin's DNA has already fused with the organic matter that was in his stomach, and mutation has begun.

As the genetic code in the pork bonds with his brain cells, we enter Justin's mind:

To see images of a slaughterhouse . . . where hogs are butchered to make sausages . . .

And now the memories are part of Justin.

In the hospital, the orderly starts to hose off the body.

He stares in amazement as Justin's burns heal before his eyes.

Then Justin *sits up*.

"Help . . ."

"Easy, man! I'll get a doctor!"

"Please . . ." He takes the orderly's

hand. "You're warm . . . Help me. I need . . ."

"What?"

"I need to know . . . everything."

Justin puts the orderly's fingers into his mouth . . .

And bites them off!

Justin is back from the dead—and hungry for knowledge.

After ingesting the orderly's memories, he understands the layout of the hospital. He dumps the body into a vat of acid, and finds his way out.

The next morning, Stacey arrives for work at Olympia Chemical.

She goes to the lab . . .

To see Justin sitting at his desk, as if nothing has happened.

He doesn't remember everything that occurred last night, only bits and pieces. All he knows is that he was in an accident, woke up in a hospital, found his way out and walked home.

When Marston passes the door to the lab, he can't believe his eyes.

He calls Justin into his office.

"How much do you know?"

"Not much."

Marston is relieved.

CALIFORNIA GOTHIC

"It must have been shock, catalepsy . . . Go see Dr. Winter, my personal physician. Let me know the results of the EEG. Then—take some time off."

Marston doesn't understand what's happened, but he's afraid that Justin will remember about the building site, and what brought him there last night.

Tonight Justin is on time for dinner.

At Stacey's apartment, he's different somehow. Changed. She doesn't know why. But she likes it.

She's made his favorite, beef bourguignon. He takes a bite . . .

And instantly absorbs the genetic contents of the food.

He remembers an abattoir, where cattle were slaughtered . . .

"Justin, are you all right?"

He finishes the bite of beef and swallows.

"Excuse me. I'm not myself."

Later, when they make love, he is rough, forceful. He's not the Justin she knew—but it turns her on.

"Mmm, don't stop . . ."

"I want you," he tells her. "To be one with you. To know everything you know . . ."

His teeth break the skin on her shoulder, and he tastes her blood.

He ingests her DNA. Now he knows everything she knows . . .

Including the contents of the company's mainframe computer.

As Stacey digs her fingernails into his back, a glowing drop of *yellow-green liquid* oozes out of the scratch . . .

The next day, at the building site, the cement mixers are ready to pour the foundations.

Justin drives up in a new company car.

Ben, the Construction Manager, is shocked to see Justin alive. He ducks into the trailer. But Justin follows.

"Mr. Travis! I heard about the accident. Welcome back . . ."

"From the dead?"

"No, I didn't mean . . ."

"This wasn't really a landfill, was it? The ground was safe—before we started."

"What are you talking about?"

But Justin knows now. The construction company locates land, Olympia moves in to test it, finds it unsafe, and condemns the property—whether it's contaminated or not. If it isn't, Olympia poisons the soil first so that the owners will sell cheap.

Olympia and the construction company both make money. It's a scam.

Ben picks up the phone to call Marston. "You can't go shooting off your mouth—"

Justin slams the phone down.

Ben takes a pistol out of the desk drawer.

Justin starts toward him.

The gun goes off . . .

And a hole appears in Justin's chest. Oozing a yellow-green liquid.

"You can't kill me," Justin tells him. "You did that already."

Then Justin bites his nose off.

He gains Ben's memories, and his suspicions are confirmed.

The memory of Marston signaling Ben as Justin drove away last night . . .

Ben following Justin, running him off the road and into the chemical truck . . .

When the crew breaks for lunch, Justin drags Ben's body outside to a fresh cement foundation, and throws him in.

Back at the Olympia offices, Justin heads for Marston's door.

He knows everything that Ben knew.

Including the fact that it was Marston who ordered Ben to have him killed.

"Justin! I thought I told you to take some time off."

"I don't need a vacation."

"Is your memory coming back?"

"One piece at a time."

"I've really got to go . . ."

"Yes, you do."

Justin advances on Marston.

"So you know," Marston says. "What do you want? Money?"

"I want to see you stopped. Before you kill anyone else."

"And you think you can do it like this? It's too big. We're building an empire. After me . . ."

Suddenly the door opens.

A beautiful young woman is standing there.

"Oh, sorry, Daddy! I didn't know you were in a meeting."

Marston introduces her. "My daughter, Shannon. The heir to the empire."

Now Justin sees the big picture.

There's more to it than he thought. Killing Marston would get him revenge. But it wouldn't bring down the company. And that's what he really wants.

In the weeks that follow, Justin spends

CALIFORNIA GOTHIC

less time with Stacey—and more with the boss's daughter.

Shannon went to business school back East, so that she can take over when Marston retires. She's shrewd, ambitious . . .

Like Justin.

The only catch is, she's engaged.

Her fiancé is a polo player named Greg. He has the right breeding. He'll fit in with her plans, and become the new Vice President of Olympia Chemical.

Getting rid of him is no problem.

Justin finds him in the barn after a polo match, and beats him to death with his own mallet.

While he's at it, he tastes Greg's blood.

And learns how to walk the walk.

At the next board meeting, Shannon raises her hand.

"Daddy?"

"Yes, dear?"

"I've brought someone with me this morning. I think you'll like what he has to say."

"Who?"

She ushers Justin into the office.

The old man is enraged. "Shannon . . . !"

"Hear him out, Daddy. Please?"

When Justin walks in, he's almost unrecognizable. He has adopted Greg's style: slicked-back hair, a three-piece suit, a power tie. His eyes are more purposeful than ever, burning with a cold fire.

He sits down opposite Marston, and begins.

"Ladies and gentlemen, the name of the game is power. And the media have that power. I propose a PR blitz. Ad time, television interviews . . . Give the people bread and circuses, if that's what it takes. Just be sure that everyone's watching the grand opening of Olympia Estates."

The board members applaud.

Marston is red-faced.

Justin has assumed control of the meeting.

No one notices when Justin scratches the side of his face . . . and his ear drops off. He's beginning to rot inside.

There's not much time left.

Justin reaches casually under the table, finds a wad of chewing gum, and uses it to stick his ear back into place.

As the applause continues.

As the opening draws near, Justin and Shannon slip away to Palm Springs for the weekend.

CALIFORNIA GOTHIC

They soak up the sun at poolside. But Justin's dead-white skin does not tan.

When Shannon starts to peel, she jumps into the water.

Justin dives in after her . . .

And a crack appears on his chest—oozing yellow-green liquid.

"Look, Mommy," says a little boy, "that man peed in the water!"

"Shush, that's not nice . . ."

"But he did!"

Justin quickly gets out of the pool.

Back in the room, he lies on the bed as if dead.

Shannon comes in and tries to rouse him, but it doesn't work. Not even when she strips off her bathing suit to get his attention.

"What's the matter with you? Don't you want me?"

Justin finally reaches for her.

"I want your warmth," he says. "I want to know all about you, everything . . ."

"Ow! Your skin is cold!"

As he moves over her, a maggot crawls out of his nose, wriggles free and drops onto her stomach.

She screams and tries to get away. When she rakes him with her fingernails, the scratches ooze yellow-green liquid.

"What is going *on* here . . . ?"

She turns on the bedside lamp.

He turns it off—as the light from the bulb shines through his hand. The bones inside clearly visible. The veins withered and dark.

"Answer me!" she says. "Do you have some kind of fucking disease or something? *What are you?*"

"I'm your conscience," he says, covering her mouth before she can scream again. "And you're the All-American Girl . . ."

He lowers his head to her.

When he raises his face again, his mouth is covered with blood.

Opening night:

The construction site has been transformed into a media circus.

A carnival flashes in the background, complete with thrill rides, as TV cameras cover the event. This was Justin's plan, a way to attract publicity.

On the bandstand, the Mayor is about to cut the ribbon, while Marston smiles for the photographers.

"This great company," the Mayor is saying, "that has done so much for our fair city . . ."

Now Justin mounts the platform.

CALIFORNIA GOTHIC

Marston whispers to him. "How was Palm Springs? Don't lie to me. I know you two were there."

"An educational experience."

Marston can't tolerate the idea of his daughter with Justin. But what can he do about it? Justin knows enough to destroy the company. It's blackmail.

"Just don't think you're going to marry the boss's daughter. That's too much!"

"It's too late for that," says Justin. "I'm not going to wait any longer."

"Where's Shan?"

"She's with you in spirit."

Now it's time for the first ride on the Cyclone Racer, a roller coaster that has been erected for the occasion.

The Mayor offers Marston the front seat.

"Go ahead," says Justin. "Don't be afraid. I'll be right next to you, all the way."

The roller coaster starts up the rickety track.

As they near the top, Justin takes a paper bag out of his coat pocket. It contains a bottle of the glowing yellow-green liquid, the chemicals that made him what he is. He unscrews the cap, takes a swig . . .

Then pours the rest of it over the safety

belt that holds them in their seats. The webbing sizzles and dissolves.

"What are you doing?" says Marston. "We'll both be killed!"

"It's time to do your part, Bob. After tonight, Olympia is finished. Now smile. The whole world is watching."

"No!"

The car goes over the top.

At the last second, Marston jumps out onto a catwalk.

Justin sees this, but there's no time to follow.

The car starts down . . .

And into an upside-down loop.

Justin is thrown out of the car. He falls and hits the ground with terrific force, as the crowd screams.

Up on the catwalk, Marston waves to show everyone that he's all right.

Below, Justin's eyes pop open.

His bones are broken. Yellow-green slime is leaking out of his cracked skull.

But that's not enough to stop him.

He starts climbing back up the scaffold, hand-over-hand, with superhuman strength and determination. The will of the living dead.

He claws his way to the top . . .

"Who are you?" cries Marston.

"Don't you get it?" says Justin. "I'm you!"

He grapples with Marston . . .

And *rips his face off*.

Then he lifts Marston over his head.

As he raises his arms, his clothes split open, eaten by the yellow-green acid that is now dripping out of his body. His ribs tear away from his chest, revealing the rot inside. Lightning flashes, illuminating Justin from behind so that for a second he is translucent—exposing the decay under the skin.

He hurls Marston down like a rag doll.

"Listen to me!" he shouts, standing on the track. "Your leaders are not what you think they are . . ."

Below, the crowd scatters.

But one person steps forward.

It's Stacey.

"Justin!"

He hears her voice, and hesitates.

"Justin, please . . . !"

At that moment, a security guard takes out his gun and fires. The bullets thwack into Justin's decomposing flesh, spraying gobs of yellow-green slime into the air.

He staggers under the impact, but stays upright.

"Listen . . . !" he shouts again.

He doesn't notice the roller coaster car, still careening on its course around the track. It zips through the last revolution, slows . . .

And starts rolling backward, covering the same route in reverse. Gaining speed. Returning to the place where it started.

The passengers scream . . .

As the car hits Justin, grinding him under its wheels and cutting him apart. His yellow-green blood splatters over the back of the Mayor's head and into his lap.

The crowd screams and runs for the exit, as Justin's body parts rain down . . .

One person is walking against the crowd. Stacey.

She is strangely calm, moving like a sleepwalker among the pieces of his body.

She comes upon Justin's severed head in the grass. Weeping silently, she leans down, picks it up . . .

And kisses it on the lips.

As she pulls away, a single thin strand hangs on the air between them, connecting his lips to hers.

Then she gently places the head back on the ground and walks away . . .

As the residue of yellow-green slime on her lips begins to glow faintly, throbbing—as if alive!

CALIFORNIA GOTHIC

"Want to see the credits?"

"I already have 'em," said Eddie. "From *Shock Zone*."

Tommy pointed his remote control at the VCR and thumbed the MUTE button. Then he hit STOP and REVERSE and began rewinding the tape.

"Nice photography, huh? All that Panaglide . . ."

"The prosthetics suck," said Eddie, closing his notepad.

"Like when?"

"Like in the hotel room. In the long shot, you can't see any cracks in his skin. And the latex is starting to peel off."

"I was looking at Shannon's tits, myself."

Eddie laughed. "She's wearing flesh-colored pasties."

"Not in the close-up."

"That's a body double."

"No way!"

"Freeze-frame it. You'll see. It looks like Michelle Bauer."

"How many times have you watched this picture?"

"As many as you," said Eddie.

"Tommy?"

"Yeah, Mom?" Tommy quickly ejected the cassette and stashed it under his pillow.

73

Eddie heard footsteps in the hall, coming closer.

The bedroom door opened.

"Are you boys still here?" Tommy's mother was a slight, stoop-shouldered woman with an uncommonly kind face. She hovered at the threshold, her fingers playing nervously over the doorknob, as though she had ventured into alien territory. "Hello, Edward," she said warmly. "How are you?"

"Hi, Mrs. Oshidari. I'm fine."

"Tommy, I thought you were going to the movies."

"We are," said Tommy, slipping into his typical thirteen-year-old persona as smoothly as if it were a glove. "We were just looking at MTV."

At the moment, however, Tommy's TV screen showed a woman in a black negligée reclining on a daybed, one long, painted fingernail poised over the buttons of a speakerphone. It was *Ask Livia*, a viewer call-in show on the local public access channel. Eddie looked at the ceiling and tried not to laugh.

Tommy aimed the remote with practiced nonchalance and scanned the dial till he found a music video.

"Your brother's waiting . . ."

"I know. Sorry, Mom."

"Well, he won't wait much longer."

CALIFORNIA GOTHIC

"Be right there," said Tommy, punching the OFF button. "I just gotta get my jacket."

"I'll expect you home by six, then. Would Edward like to stay for dinner?"

"No, thanks, Mrs. Oshidari."

"Say hello to your mother for me, will you, please?" She started to close the door in a series of diminishing increments that might never reach zero.

"I will."

"I'll tell Mike you're on your way," she said to Tommy.

At last the door closed all the way.

They waited a few seconds, then cracked up.

"Busted!" said Eddie.

"No way. She can't see without her glasses." Tommy withdrew the tape from under his pillow and sheathed it in an empty cassette box for *The WWF Presents: Wrestling's Greatest Bleeps, Bloopers and Bodyslams*.

"*Six* o'clock?" said Eddie.

"I'll use the pay phone at the mall," said Tommy, "and tell her we missed the first show. That way we can catch *Ninja Cop*, too."

"What does she think we're going to see?"

"*Return to Fern Gully.*"

Eddie groaned.

"What was I supposed to tell her? *American Zombie II* is R-rated."

"My folks know. My dad, at least. He likes horror films."

Eddie regretted saying it as soon as the words were out of his mouth. Tommy's father had been dead for only six months. But his friend did not flinch.

"Anyway, thanks for showing me Part One again."

"No es problema." Tommy finished tying his tennis shoes and reached for his windbreaker. "It's a classic. Are you going to compare them in your column?"

"Maybe. If Part Two holds up."

Tommy slung his windbreaker over his shoulder and waited for Eddie to roll off the bed and join him at the door. "What's the plot this time?"

Eddie tried to remember the summary from *Shock Zone*. "Let's see. Shannon comes back from the dead and takes over the company. But Stacey turns into a zombie, too, and fights her for control. It's the return of the murdered girlfriend, versus the woman he really loved."

"Which one wins?"

Eddie grinned slyly. "That's the biggie, isn't it?"

Chapter Four

As Markham backed out of the driveway, shadows like black spiderwebs moved over the hood of the car. Then he was rolling out from under the trees and down the street, the sun glancing off his windshield.

He lowered the visor and checked the rearview mirror. The front of his house was a weathered face, the door a mouth, the windows glazed eyes. Behind one of those eyes, was Evie watching?

I didn't say good-bye, he thought.

At the corner, the mail truck screaked to a stop. He pulled up behind it and waited to see which way it would go. When it turned right he cut left across the intersection, heading out as quickly as possible in the opposite direction.

He made another left immediately, but still he felt eyes on his back.

There was the school, the empty playground,

the louvered windows glaring hotly. One side of the cafeteria was now defiled with gang writing, lines so stylized and peculiar that they might be deciphered only in reverse, like da Vinci's notebooks. He had never noticed them before; perhaps they had appeared during the night, in the manner of crop circles. He reached up, centering a fragment of the message in his mirror, but it remained unreadable.

He drove on.

When his tongue began to itch, he told himself that it was the Santa Ana wind.

It came every year, a sign that the seasons were changing. There were no real seasons here, only a shift in emphasis, an adjustment in the number of daylight hours. With the warm March wind, people put away cotton sweaters and made plans for long days at Disneyland and the beach, teenagers found creative new ways to test the limits, and restless children simply refused to stay down for the count, as if in training for summer vacation. Then the wind moved on and the climate entered a holding pattern until June or July, when the real heat waves started. But for now, in the month of May, the tease was on.

He crossed the railroad tracks.

Should he try to catch up with Eddie, offer him a lift? He looked down the boulevard, past

CALIFORNIA GOTHIC

the lumberyard and the gate to the Pick-A-Part lot, but did not see his son.

He kept driving.

He cruised by Fatburger's, the Weenie Wigwam drive-thru, Los Tacos Locos and El Pollo Muerto, all built practically adjacent to one another, their signs arranged like movie marquees to lure him in. He had no appetite. Then, at the end of the block, he spotted Reggae Rat's Cheesy Pizza Parlor.

They served beer, didn't they?

He gripped the wheel so hard that he heard his knuckles crack, and steered instead into the Builder's Bonanza lot.

He wandered the aisles for several minutes before he remembered why he had stopped. He wove through a maze of rubber trash cans, discounted lawn furniture, barbecue grills and ice chests, looking for the paint and brushes. In the Plumbing Department, water-saving showerheads recoiled against the wall like cobras ready to spit in his eye. The Electrical Department contained enough spooled wire to detonate the neighborhood from miles away. Unfinished bookcases and home entertainment centers offered corners where one might hide, if only their sliding doors and drop panels were in place. At the Information Booth, a clerk showed a weekend tinkerer how to arm a smoke detector with batteries the size of shotgun cartridges.

Markham found his way to the Garden Annex, where young couples loaded spring flowers and bags of fertilizer into shopping carts, and felt beads of sweat popping out on his forehead. He turned around, hoping to spot an exit.

A saleswoman with a short, efficient haircut approached him.

"May I help you, sir?"

"Uh, no, I . . ."

He squinted down at the ID badge pinned to her ill-fitting, oversized uniform. Was it really blank, or would a name appear if he stared long enough?

"Sir, are you all right?"

"A drink," he said. "Where can I get a—?"

"Right over there." She pointed to a water-cooler in the corner, under the insecticides.

He pushed past her and fled, the letter in his shirt pocket pressing against his chest.

He parked behind the bookstore. From what he could see through the back door, there were no customers inside. Not a good sign, but for once it made him feel better.

Katie was busy restocking the Young Adult section, while Len nodded over the telephone, the coiled cord disturbing layers of paperwork spread out on the counter. When Len heard the bell he glanced up, shrugged and gave Markham a curious smile.

CALIFORNIA GOTHIC

"Hi, Dan," said Katie from the top of the ladder. "Can't stay away, huh?"

Markham acknowledged her, then held Len's gaze and hooked a thumb toward the back room.

"Let me put you on hold," Len said into the phone, "while I check."

He slipped out from behind the counter and followed Markham down the aisle.

"What are you looking for?" called Katie.

"A first printing of *Autumn Angels*," said Len.

"We used to have one," she said. "Will they settle for *An East Wind Coming*?"

"Why don't you ask?"

"Oh, Dan? When do you want to appraise the Birdwell collection?"

"Later," Markham told her.

"I know. But somebody came in about it. His daughter, I think . . ."

"Later, I said."

Len went with him into the office.

Immediately Markham closed the door and began moving boxes.

"What's up?" asked Len.

"Did you get the beer?"

Len looked at him blankly through wire-rimmed glasses. "What beer?"

"The Heinekens. For the Bradbury signing."

"Not yet."

Markham sat on the edge of the desk, breathing heavily. His skin was tingling as though ants were crawling up his arms, and his lips were so dry they were splitting.

"Why not?"

"Hey, it's a week away." Len flashed his teeth, waiting to catch the joke. "What's the matter, Danny, you want one?"

Markham slumped into his chair.

Len stopped grinning. "My God, you do." He made sure the door was closed all the way. "What happened?"

Markham took out his wallet and started flipping through the business cards and phone numbers. "How's your wife?" he said tightly.

"Jean? She's okay. Why?"

"I have a question for you, Len. Do you tell her everything?"

"Like what?"

"Do you ever lie to her?"

"Sure," said Len, playing along. "What she's getting for her birthday. How many times her mother called. That sort of thing."

"Anything else?"

"Let me see. No. Yeah, sometimes, I guess. What's your point?"

"I've never lied to Evie." He thought of the times when the business dropped off to nothing, and the angina pains, the real reason Dr. Bowker had put him on the medication last year: "I may not mention some things . . ."

CALIFORNIA GOTHIC

"Ah, the sin of omission," said Len with a twinkle in his eye.

"But if she asks me a direct question, I tell her. It's a principle. I don't want to start lying now."

"What did she ask you?"

"Nothing."

"But you're afraid she might . . . Hmm. Know what I think? I think you want to tell her, whatever it is, before she asks. That way you won't have to guilt-trip yourself."

Markham did not say anything.

"So go ahead. Confession is good for the soul." Len must have had second thoughts, because he added, "What is it? You don't have a girlfriend, do you?"

"I used to."

"When?"

"I lived with someone, right after college."

"So?"

Again Markham remained silent.

"When's the last time you saw her?"

"A long time ago."

Len chuckled. "So you've been fantasizing about her with Evie . . ."

"She's dead."

"Oh. Sorry, man."

"It's been seventeen years. She poured gasoline over herself and lit a match."

"Jesus."

There was a tap on the door and Katie stuck her head in, all golden curls and unblemished skin.

"Did you find *Autumn Angels*?"

"Not yet," said Len.

"Well, that woman on line one—"

Len tried to give her a sign. "Not now, Katie."

"What should I tell her?"

"I'll take care of it," said Markham.

"Okay?" Len said to her.

"Okay, boys. I get it. This is a private conversation. Ex-cuse me!" Katie withdrew, easing the door shut.

The red light was still blinking on the extension. Markham picked up the receiver and punched line one.

"Try Dangerous Visions," he said, "in Sherman Oaks. No, I don't have the number."

He broke the connection.

Then he said to Len, "Do you remember the CSR?"

Len rubbed his chin. "Didn't they used to play with Neil Young?"

"The Church of Satan the Redeemer."

"Oh, yeah. It was some kind of revolutionary thing, like the Symbionese Liberation Army. Right?"

Markham nodded. "When it got out of hand, the cops burned them to the ground."

CALIFORNIA GOTHIC

"They should have had Patty Hearst with them."

"That didn't save the SLA."

Len took off his glasses and cleaned them studiously on his T-shirt, frowning. "What are you telling me? That you had a girlfriend in the Church?"

"We lived together for four years. Then she left me, and joined them."

Len sat on a dusty carton from Borderlands Press, full of shrink-wrapped books. "I didn't know," he said.

"Nobody does. The court sealed the files."

"Not even Evie?"

Markham shook his head.

"So why tell her now?"

Markham felt the letter against his chest, threatening to unfold. He took it out of his shirt pocket and set it on the desk like an origami bird.

"This came in the mail today."

Len handled it with care, as if it were a page from a rare manuscript.

" 'Jude'?" he said when he had finished reading it.

"Judy Rios," said Markham.

"How do you know?"

"She was the only Jude I ever met. At least that was what I called her."

"No shit." Len wagged his head, stunned.

"The one who burned herself, instead of going to prison. I remember now."

"I always wondered what it was like for her, a second before she struck the match. Sometimes I still have nightmares about it."

"Who the hell sent this?"

"That's what I'd like to know."

"I thought they got them all."

"I thought so, too."

"Then it's a hoax. Somebody followed the case, read all the books . . ."

"My name's not in any of the books."

"Well, somebody figured it out. Some sick son of a bitch." Len pushed the note away with distaste. "You should turn this over to the FBI."

"Why, if it's a hoax? And what do I tell them, that a dead woman wrote me a letter?"

"You don't think that, do you?"

"I'm not crazy, Lenny. I saw the photographs of her body."

"Then you don't have anything to worry about."

They avoided each other's eyes for a moment.

Len stood and walked over to the desk, picked up the letter and tore it into tiny pieces.

"Some sick son of a bitch out there."

It was good to hear Len say it again.

"Yeah," said Markham.

He fingered the slips of paper he had dumped out of his wallet. Now they were mixed in with

CALIFORNIA GOTHIC

the pieces of the letter. He moved them around on the desk, sorting them, and noticed the scrap he had been looking for. It was old and creased and rubbed brown from having been carried around for so long.

"Thanks, Len."

"For what?"

"See you out front. I want to sit here for a few minutes."

"Take your time. This is your day off."

"Right."

Len hesitated at the door. "If you're thinking about bringing flowers home for Evie, take my advice: don't. Then she *will* know that something's wrong, and you'll end up telling her everything. Which you don't want to do, because there's no point to it."

"How about if I take her out tonight?"

"Perfect. Dinner and a movie. Your boy, too. A family affair."

"He's already at the movies."

"He's got the right idea."

"Anyway, I should look at the Birdwell estate tonight."

"Will you forget that? Katie and I can do it."

"She doesn't have a date?"

"She does now." Lenny was finally grinning again as he closed the door behind him.

The office felt cold, insulated with so many cartons of books. Now that Len was gone they seemed to press in on him, as if he were barricaded against the outside world. Had it been this way for the last scruffy members of the CSR, hiding in that tenement basement, when the S.W.A.T. team moved in? He thought of her there among the boxes, the others all dead or dying from bullet wounds, and the can of gasoline, and the match. Then the spark and the roar. He saw skin bubbling and melting off bone and the bones toppling forward into the flames, heard the squeal of sizzling flesh . . .

He squeezed his eyes shut, trying to make the flames stop.

When he opened his eyes, he saw the folded slip of paper under his fingers.

There was a name and number written on it.

He lifted the phone and dialed.

"Hello?" said a man's voice.

Markham felt himself faltering but went ahead with it. "Hello, uh—" He managed to read the handwriting. "Bill?"

"Yes?"

"You don't know me. I got your number from . . . a friend. In case I ever needed it."

"Glad you called. What's your name?"

Markham's throat tightened so that he could not answer.

"Well," the man went on, "my name's Bill, and I'm an alcoholic."

"Hi, Bill. This is . . ."

CALIFORNIA GOTHIC

Markham pushed the pieces of the letter into a pile on his desk. A hoax, he thought. That's all. He hadn't even known any of them. And now they were dead, just as she was. The fingerprints . . . there was no doubt about it.

"My—my name's Dan. I'm an alcoholic, too." He felt funny saying it, after so long.

"Hi, Dan."

"But I'm okay. Really."

"Sure? We can talk about it, if you want . . ."

"I'm sure."

He hung up.

Then he swept the pieces off the desk and into the wastebasket.

Three customers came into the store before he left, but he did not wait around to see what they wanted.

On the way home traffic was light, the sky as blue-white and iridescent as leaded crystal held up to the sun. The fragrance of roasted pork and lemon-basted chicken blew along the boulevard. Families poured into Reggae Rat's, laughing and holding hands, for Saturday afternoon pizza and soft drinks. Dogs ran free. A man on the radio was talking about being and nothingness. Markham recognized it as one of the lectures by Alan Watts from the Pacifica Archives, always worth hearing again. But for the moment he felt that he knew all he wanted to know about form and formlessness, yin and yang, being and nonbeing and the dynamics of change. Without guilt he tuned down the dial from KPFK to KPCC. It was time to listen to some jazz. The hot, dry wind had moved on.

Evie's car was in the driveway. He parked behind her as John Handy's tenor saxophone soared and lilted through the same twelve bars one last time. Then he shut it off and went inside.

The front door was locked.

Why, if she was home?

"Evie?"

He walked through the living room. Now, with the sun well past its zenith, the windows were shaded by the eaves; the effect was dark and comfortable. He listened for her, then crossed to the bookcases that stood like pillars protecting the rest of the house. Was she on the back porch? He remembered a lot of laundry in the basket, waiting to be washed.

"Honey?"

She was not there, either. He was about to go into the kitchen, when he noticed the yard.

Where's my tree? he thought.

He imagined Evie wielding a chain saw, cutting through the old growth with reckless abandon. Couldn't she wait?

The tree was there. It was split down the mid-

CALIFORNIA GOTHIC

dle as if by lightning, the branches splayed across the path to the garage.

The wind?

No, dry rot, he thought. I should have soaked it. I was always going to. But I never did.

Had she been hurt?

"Evie!"

He ran through the house, and found her in the bedroom.

She was curled up, asleep, with the sheet over her head. The tent, they called it on Sunday mornings.

The shape was not quite right.

Where were her legs?

He touched the edge of the covers.

Her hair looked darker. The back of her neck was moist—that was it. She was fevered, perspiring under the covers in his heavy robe. She lay on her side, knees drawn up, in a fetal position.

Sleeping in the middle of the afternoon?

"Honey . . . ?"

She twitched at his touch and the sound of his voice, and turned over with frightening speed.

Her face was not the same. The eyes appeared dull, filmed over, as if covered by a transparent inner membrane. She was not really asleep but only dazed, suspended in a waking dream.

"Are you all right?"

She rolled quickly against him.

Incredibly, she was shivering.

"Oh, Danny . . ."

"I saw the backyard. What happened?"

She held him tightly. "The tree," she said, remembering, as if it did not matter now. "It was the wind . . ."

"Don't worry, I'll take care of it."

"Danny, I had a dream. It was awful."

He rubbed her back through the thick robe, then pushed her away and looked at her. He wanted to see her face.

Did she know?

How?

Well, if she did, if she had sensed something was wrong and so lain here imagining the worst, he could dispel all that now with the right words. He wanted her to know that there was nothing to worry about.

"Evie," he began, "I got a letter."

She looked at him uncomprehendingly.

"It's not important, but I wanted to tell you anyway. Somebody's playing a joke on us."

"What letter?"

Maybe she didn't know. Too late. He forced himself to smile, as if it really was funny. "A long time ago, before I met you, I knew this girl . . ."

"What did she look like?"

"It doesn't matter."

CALIFORNIA GOTHIC

"I want to know."

She seemed serious. "Evie, I can hardly remember . . ."

"Tell me!"

"Well, she was sort of thin—skinny, actually—with long hair. What's the difference?"

"She cut her hair off, didn't she?"

Suddenly his heart began to beat faster.

"I guess so." Right before she moved out, he thought. "So what? Evie, she died years ago, and . . ."

Evie shook her head. "That's wrong."

"What do you mean?" He felt his blood pressure increase, throbbing behind his eyes. "What I'm trying to tell you is, she's dead. She committed suicide. She—"

"No, she didn't," said Evie. *"She was here."*

Chapter Five

I'd better move before it's too late, thought Evie as she lay there listening to the chain saw.

Her toes uncurled as she straightened one leg, the sheet scraping against her like a coarse wool blanket. It was a miracle she could move even this much.

A dream, that's all, she had told Dan, and after a while he'd believed her and loosened his arms; and now he was outside, clearing away the tree with his power tools. She heard the scream of metal teeth ripping through soft wood, then the plop of a severed branch falling away.

Where was Eddie?

She lowered an arm, sweeping the rest of the sheet aside as if peeling off a layer of skin. The air rushed over her and the blood tingled painfully in her veins. Another limb fell and struck the ground, and the chain saw sputtered and stopped. She dangled her legs over the edge and forced herself to stand.

Her right side was numb from lying so long in one position. She locked her knee and tried to make it work. Then she balanced by the bathroom door while sensation returned, her tissues expanding like a sponge full of blood and broken glass. Her shorts and top were still by the tub. She pulled them on, but decided they wouldn't do—they left too much of her body exposed to the air. She peered into the closet. Where was her long-sleeved blouse?

On her way to the back porch, she passed Eddie's room.

It was not as she remembered it. What had become of the scattered papers, the magazines, the clumped socks on the floor? There were the shapes of his desk and chair, but now hidden under plastic sheeting as though wrapped for indefinite storage. Even his bed was covered like an oxygen tent in an intensive care ward. How long had it been vacant?

I'm already too late, she thought.

She heard the back door open and close, and then heavy footsteps behind her.

"Ev? How are you feeling?"

She knew what that meant. Dan wanted to know if she was all right; if not he would insist that she stay, perhaps even restrain her. She

CALIFORNIA GOTHIC

tensed, waiting for the rough touch of his hands on her arms.

"Fine."

She felt the heat of his body. Why was there the smell of the earth on him? Had he been digging again? She moved quickly out of his grasp.

"You look a little shaky," he said.

"I had a bad dream. But I'm okay now."

"You had me worried."

"I said I'm okay. How's the tree?"

"The tree?" He seemed to have trouble with the change in subjects. "It's a total loss. For now, I'm cutting it down to the soil line. Looks like we're going to have a lot of firewood."

"That's nice," she said. She turned and went to the clothes basket on the porch. "Have you seen my white jumpsuit?"

"No. Why?"

"I need it."

"Maybe you sent it to the cleaners."

Was he lying to keep her here?

She rummaged in the basket, then saw her black stretch Levi's and flowered print blouse draped over the washing machine. They were wrinkled, but there was nothing she could do about that now. She stepped into the Levi's, leaning against the wall for support, and buttoned them over her shorts. Then she pulled the blouse on over her tank top.

"Why are you getting dressed?"
"I have to go out."
"Now?"
"I was supposed to meet Jean."
"A little late for that, isn't it?"
"I just called her," she lied. "She's waiting." She tucked in her blouse and started around him.
"Evie?"
"I'm in a hurry."
"Don't you think we should talk?"
"About what?"
"The girl."
"What girl?"
"The one who came to the door."
"It was a *dream*, Dan."
"All of it?"
"Yes."
"But I thought you said . . ."
She led him through the house. At the front door she asked, "Where are my car keys?"
"Where did you put them?"
"I don't know. Give me yours."
He reached into his jeans. "Honey, are you sure . . . ?"
"I won't be long."
She looked at him, at the dirt on his face, on his shirt. *What have you been digging?* The question caught in her throat.
If I ask him, what will happen?

CALIFORNIA GOTHIC

"Where's Eddie?" she said, as casually as possible.

"He went over to Tommy's. Remember?"

"Of course I remember." She took the cold, hard keys from his hand and left him standing there. "Well, see you in a while."

Then she toed into her flats and clicked down the steps to the driveway.

When she started the car, the radio crackled. It was one of Dan's stations—a string orchestra, but ruined by a cheap, honking saxophone that couldn't find the right notes. Why can't he just play the melody? she thought irritably, and switched it off.

She backed down the driveway, spun the wheel till the power steering stuttered and skipped as if she were dragging a child under the tires. In the mirror the other front yards were neat and empty, without bicycles or toys. There were no children on this street. She tromped the gas and lurched away from the curb, laying down black lines.

At the intersection, she did not see any pedestrians in either direction. Halfway up the next block a man loaded a body bag onto a truck. No, it was only a gardener, struggling to lift a bundle of grass cuttings into the back of his pickup. She turned left without waiting for the light to change and drove toward Bradfield.

The clock on the dashboard had to be broken. How could it be 2:30 already?

She fought to contain her fear. Of what? There was no time to sort through her feelings in an orderly fashion, not now. She knew only that her life had been secure—until a few hours ago, when the bell rang and she opened the front door. Now she felt the chaos around her, moving on a restless wind that threatened to uproot and rearrange it all. Order was the illusion, she understood at last. Houses, cars, the grid of streets, the laws and regulations that desperately frightened people had invented—none of it added up to anything more than a primitive circle of wagons around a campfire. There were dark waves of chance ready to blow everything away at any moment. It had always been just outside the door, waiting to get in; how foolish to think that there could be any real defense.

As she prepared to make a right turn onto Bradfield, she spotted a group of teenagers near the railroad tracks.

She decided to take a closer look.

Drawing even with them, she rolled her window down and heard their high, hoarse laughter. There were three girls and two boys. The girls were bare-legged, their figures concealed

CALIFORNIA GOTHIC

by oversized T-shirts, and each had unnaturally shiny hair arranged in identical fashion, as if they all had the same model's photograph taped to their bedroom mirrors at home.

Evie pulled over and idled, and watched them stumble across to the tracks.

She saw that the boys were gangly and flat-footed, with long shirts and baseball caps worn backwards.

They were both older than Eddie.

She dropped into gear and drove on parallel with the tracks, waiting for the next corner so that she could get back to Bradfield.

The Oshidaris lived in a sprawling, ranch-style house from the fifties, with a winding flagstone walk, a dichondra lawn and immaculately trimmed hedges. Evie had forgotten how much nicer it was than her own. As she parked in front of the split rail fence and made her way around the station wagon in the driveway, she glanced back at Dan's Toyota and noticed how dirty it was, the windshield with two arcs of clear glass showing, cut clean by the wipers, like two dark eyes watching her. Had she locked it?

"Welcome!" said a voice.

"Hello . . . ?"

"So you think you know where your children

are?" It was a man, inside the house. *"Watching a movie while you're in bed—safe, right?"*

Beyond the gate in the fence, a door opened and a woman backed out of the kitchen, dragging a black plastic bag.

"Excuse me," said Evie.

"WRONG!"

The bag was filled to bursting with something heavy and unwieldy. The woman got it over the threshold, then began sliding it up the driveway, toward the garage.

"What they're watching may be violent . . . pornographic . . . or even SATANIC!"

The voice came from a television set in the kitchen, Evie realized. One of those afternoon tabloid shows. She recognized the voice as that of an actor who had once starred in a TV series about motorcycle cops. What was his name? He had had a lot of teeth.

"And all because of Digital Masking! Secret messages that can be added to ANY videotape . . . to warp young minds!"

"Mrs. Oshidari?"

She can't hear me because of that damned TV, thought Evie, and unlatched the gate.

"Is it possible? Experts say yes! If you're a mother who cares about your child . . ."

"Oh!"

The woman flinched and let go of the bag

CALIFORNIA GOTHIC

when Evie touched her, glancing over her shoulder as though expecting to see a ghost.

"Sorry, I—I'm Eddie's mother."

"Eddie?" The woman's eyes were as large and black as a cat's at twilight, ready for anything. Her narrow shoulders hunched defensively.

"You know, Edward." Evie felt her heart speed up, skip a beat. "Markham. He's a friend of your son's. I've dropped him off a few times. And I believe we've spoken on the phone."

"Then you owe it to yourself to meet our special guest for today, an authority on subliminal messages . . ."

"Oh, Edward!" Mrs. Oshidari brightened, her mouth relaxing in a broad, warm smile. "Such a fine boy. He's welcome in our house anytime."

Evie relaxed a bit, too. Hearing the woman speak her son's name seemed to offer the kind of confirmation that was important to her just now. From the kitchen, an unseen audience applauded.

"I'm sorry to bother you . . ."

"Not at all. I was just doing my spring cleaning."

Evie looked at the bag. It was half as tall as Mrs. Oshidari and appeared to weigh at least as much. What was in it? Something large, lumpy and very heavy. Evie made out a long, rounded

DENNIS ETCHISON

shape at the bottom. It might have been a shoe. Was there a foot attached?

"Tommy's father," said Mrs. Oshidari.

"What?"

"The rest of his things. What the Salvation Army didn't want. Tommy was supposed to help me, but he's off to the movies again."

"Tell me," the announcer was saying, *"what do your children watch?"*

"When did he leave?"

"About an hour ago."

"And my son went with him?"

"I hope that's all right . . ."

"Science fiction and horror pictures, mostly," said a woman in the audience.

"Of course. Did they walk? To the mall, I mean."

The audience groaned disapprovingly.

"No."

"You drove them, then?" said Evie. "I would have myself, but . . ."

"Mike took them."

"Mike?"

"Tommy's brother. He has his license now."

"I see."

"Can you remember any of the titles?"

"Didn't Edward tell you where he was going?" asked Mrs. Oshidari.

"Let me see. The Hungry Dead, American Zombie . . ."

CALIFORNIA GOTHIC

"Of course he did."

"He had your permission, then?"

"Yes," said Evie. "He had my permission."

A chorus of women gasped.

Mrs. Oshidari smiled even more broadly but did not meet Evie's eyes. Overhead, something unseen moved in the trees, shaking leaves down at their feet.

"I hope we get that rain," said Mrs. Oshidari. *"Anything else?"*

"Yes," said Evie.

"That one with Freddy and Jason, what was it called?"

"Not today, of course," said Mrs. Oshidari.

"No."

Evie took a step back. A dry leaf crunched under her heel, the sound of a tiny skeleton pulverized.

"Do you know what movie they went to see?"

"I really don't. I can't keep up with them all. So much shooting and killing . . . Not my Tommy, though. Those pictures give him bad dreams."

"You're lucky," Evie muttered.

"Am I?"

"It may be a blessing in disguise."

"I see what you mean! Well, I hope you're right . . ."

"My name's Eve, by the way." She extended

her hand. "I was just in the neighborhood. I thought I'd stop by."

"I'm glad you did. I'm Dotty." She missed Evie's hand, grasped her wrist and pumped it. "I'll see that Edward calls home as soon as they get back."

She's nearsighted, thought Evie. "Would you? I'd appreciate that."

"Certainly."

"It's just . . ." She tried to think of an excuse. "We were going out tonight. I want to be sure Eddie remembers, so he won't be late. I'll pick him up."

"Mike can drive him. It's no trouble."

"That's very kind of you. We're going to dinner. With my husband. The three of us. We like to do that sometimes. As often as we can." Evie faltered. How long had it been?

"We did that, too," said Mrs. Oshidari, "when Tommy's father was alive."

Oh no, thought Evie. That was what the woman meant. The things in the bag . . . she remembered now about Tommy's father passing away. When was it? Not long, she thought, horrified. Eddie had told her but it hadn't registered. Until now. Because I was too busy to pay attention.

"I'm so sorry," said Evie.

Mrs. Oshidari's eyes focused past the driveway and the yard. "It's better this way. At least

CALIFORNIA GOTHIC

he didn't suffer. Would you care for a cup of coffee, Eve?"

"No, thank you. Really. I've got to be going." She stepped back around the gate and latched it between them. "Some other time."

"I remember now," said Mrs. Oshidari.

"Oh?"

"What they were going to see."

"We all know about R-rated films. They're bad enough. But what about PG? Even G? They're safe, right?"

"Yes?"

"It was the animated one. *Return to Fern Gully*, I think. Yes, that's it."

"Did you know they're the most dangerous of all? Thanks to Digital Masking, powerful messages can be encoded in virtually anything, even Disney movies! Let's look at some examples . . ."

"I hear that's a safe one," said Evie. "A good one, I mean." She backtracked down the driveway, and stepped into the dichondra. It squished underfoot. "Sorry, but I have to go now."

"It was lovely to meet you," said Mrs. Oshidari.

"Yes . . ."

"Come by any time."

"I will." She's lonely, thought Evie. I wish I could help her. "I promise."

DENNIS ETCHISON

* * *

There was no one at the entrance to the multiplex, so she walked in.

A college girl with hair like exploded nerve-ends stood up behind the candy counter, adjusting her uniform.

"Take your ticket over here."

"That's all right," said Evie. "I don't have one."

She scanned the lobby and the titles on the lightboxes over each door. But the lettering was too small to make out from here.

"Ma'am?"

Sweet Violation, read the first sign. Not likely, she thought, and kept walking.

"Ma'am . . . ?"

The girl caught up with her just before *Lethal Injection*, the second door. Evie ignored her and reached for the handle.

"Ma'am, you can't go in there . . ."

"I won't be long," Evie told her.

". . . Without a ticket."

"I don't need a ticket."

The girl was baffled. Then she said, "Are you on the list?"

"What list?"

"Um, the comps. Name?"

"Eve Markham."

"Just a minute. I'll check."

"Don't bother. I'm not on your list. Where's *Rain Gully?*"

"*Return to Fern Gully?* Theater Four . . ."

"Thank you," said Evie, and moved on.

Back at the candy counter there was a hurried conference, and then a young man with a military-style crewcut and a manager's nametag caught up with her at the third door. He stepped in front of Evie to block her way.

"Where are you going?" he said.

"This one. Do you mind?"

"You got to have a *ticket*," he explained elaborately, as if she were retarded or hard-of-hearing, "if you want to see the *movie*."

"I don't want to see the movie."

"No?"

"I'm looking for someone."

"So's everybody, lady. I could give a shit what you do in there, okay? But you got to pay."

"It's my son," she said.

She faced him down.

"Okay," he said, "okay. You got it. But just for a minute."

As she opened the fourth door, the air sparkled in front of her. A luminous fairy hovered onscreen, leaving a trail of magical dust in its wake. Evie walked down the short aisle, searching the heads, but the children were low in their seats, half-hidden, like rows of baby cabbages. The fairy was a tiny, pocket-sized bathing beauty with full breasts, a wasp waist and rounded hips; at the front of her glittery leotard, above a belt woven from forest-green vines, was a deep, spectacular crescent of cleavage.

"Eddie?"

Not one of the little boys took his eyes from the screen.

The young manager was waiting for her.

"Find him?"

"I will."

She skipped the fifth door and the remake of *Lolita*. She doubted if Eddie had even heard of Dustin Hoffman. In Number Six, two women sat in the back row of the otherwise empty theater, waiting for Jodie Foster's *Rubyfruit Jungle* to begin. She decided to go back to Number Three.

"Look, lady," said the manager, "what picture did he *pay* to see? Because if he doesn't have his ticket stub . . ."

"This one," she said. She read the title, *American Zombie II*, and shuddered.

"You already went in there."

"No, not yet."

"I saw you."

Was he trying to keep her from her own son?

Just then the door to Theater Three burst open and dozens of people, mostly teens,

CALIFORNIA GOTHIC

stampeded for the restrooms and the exit. A boy steered his girlfriend around the canister ash trays, one arm draped over her shoulder. His fat fingers tightened possessively, only an inch above her breast. What was wrong with his mouth? It was red and bruised, as though smeared with blood. Then two younger boys bumped into Evie. One of them paused long enough to turn back against the rush of bodies.

"*Mom?*"

She snatched Eddie's arm out of the throng and pulled him across the lobby.

"What are you doing here, Mom?"

"Come with me."

His face fell as if the flesh was melting. "But Tommy—"

"Never mind."

He jerked free long enough to make hand signals at the other boy, who lingered by the wall, attempting to blend in with the Coming Attractions posters for *Look Who's Dead* and *C.H.U.M.P.—The Movie*.

"What were you doing in there?" she snapped.

"Where?"

"Don't look so innocent," she said. "I know what you were watching."

"It's a good film," he said defiantly.

The manager followed them out.

"Ticket?"

"What ticket?" said Eddie.

"Your stub."

"I don't have it anymore."

"Here," said Evie, fishing in her purse. She handed over a ten. "This is for the both of them."

The manager accepted it wordlessly and ducked back inside, gone as quickly as a panhandler in Hare Krishna robes.

She grabbed Eddie's shoulder, pressing her thumb into the hollow by his neck. Though it must have hurt him, his expression became stony, his lips thin.

"I paid," he said.

"I don't believe you."

"Dad gave me the money. He said I could go."

"I don't believe that, either. Not for one minute."

He stared at her, his cheeks reddening. "Why don't you ask him?"

People were looking at them.

She let him go.

"See you, Tommy," Eddie said in a loud voice, making sure that everyone in the lobby heard. "She wants to *talk* to me."

He was trying to humiliate her, to make it sound as though she were the unreasonable one. But outside the theater, in the mall, crowds

CALIFORNIA GOTHIC

passed without noticing. It was as if nothing had happened. She sat down on a bench.

When she finally looked up at Eddie, his face was so tight that his eyes sparked like flint, giving off light.

"What do you want?"

"To talk to you," she said in a low voice, endeavoring to appear calm amid the bustling shoppers.

"What about?"

"I mean, I wanted to see you."

"Why?"

Now it sank in that he was all right, and the sense of urgency left her. Why had she come? There was no reason that she could put into words, at least not that he would understand.

"You didn't tell me where you were going," she said.

"Yes, I did."

He was right. But that was not the point. How to explain it?

"I just wanted to know that you were all right."

"How old do you think I am?" he said.

She saw Tommy loitering in the lobby, avoiding them both.

"I didn't mean to embarrass you," she said.

But she had. He was the one who was humiliated. In front of his friend.

"Where did you think I went? To a *bar*?"

"I know you didn't lie to me," she said. He never had. It was not in his nature. He was his father's son. *A bar?* Had he really said that? What a funny thing for him to say, funny and sweet. "I wanted to tell you that—that we're going out to dinner tonight."

"Great."

"With Daddy. Dad. He's taking us. I didn't want you to be late."

"Do I have to go home now?"

He was really playing the martyr. Her heart went out to him. She wanted to take him in her arms and kiss him but knew that he would not let her.

"Not now," she said. "I just wanted you to know."

A young couple pushed a baby cart out of Miller's Outpost and crossed around the escalators to the food court on the other side. Children in stonewashed jeans with rolled cuffs played tag along the railing. A security guard wielded a walkie talkie with a rubberized antenna and winked at a mother carrying a newborn in her arms; it could not have been more than a few weeks old. The aroma of fresh-baked chocolate chip cookies wafted up from the landing directly below, and through the skylight in the roof clear blue-white rays shone down on them all. Evie saw that the mall was filled with hu-

CALIFORNIA GOTHIC

manity on a Saturday afternoon, that was all, and she was a part of it, too. She was surrounded by the sights and sounds and smells of life, the details she had not had time to notice, and the light from overhead was warm enough even through the glass to take the chill from her arms.

"Oh, Eddie . . ." she began. "Eddie, I'm sorry." I don't know what's wrong with me, she thought. "Go on. Tommy's waiting. I'll see you about six. Do you need a ride . . . ?"

But he was already back inside the theater.

How was the movie? she wondered as she descended the escalator to the parking lot. She hoped he had liked it. There was little enough to occupy his inquisitive mind. If he found it in popular culture, that was all right. Of course it was. What had she been thinking? Later there would be high school, and then college; he'd surely get the scholarship of his choice. There was plenty of time. For now, let him act his age and enjoy it. She wouldn't want him any other way.

A bad dream, she thought. That's what it was. A real bummer.

On the way home the sky cleared, leaving a slate upon which she might write anything she liked. Yes, dinner and a movie, she thought. Like we used to. If Dan's up for it. Or maybe just dinner.

Tomorrow's Sunday and we'll sleep late. We'll lie in bed, in our tent.

She neared the stop sign on the other side of the tracks and started to roll through it, but decided not to. Another point on her driving record and the car insurance would soar. She stepped on the brake and sat there for a second, turning her head first to the right and then the left, like a responsible driver.

The tracks were empty in both directions. She wondered if they were used at all anymore. Farther down, around the junkyard, the rails were overgrown with weeds. Still, she did not like to sit on the tracks any longer than absolutely necessary. It made her feel vulnerable, a reflex acquired from news stories about cars that stalled and refused to start and got cut in half and dragged by locomotives that appeared out of nowhere. But there was no chance of that here.

She dropped into gear and started across, and was about to turn up Remar to Stewart, when she glanced in the rearview mirror.

A hundred yards behind her, back on the tracks, someone was walking between the ties, headed in the direction of the wrecking yard. There was something about the figure that made her reach up and center it in the mirror.

She slammed the brake pedal into the floor-

CALIFORNIA GOTHIC

board, ran her window down the rest of the way and leaned out, looking back.

It was the girl in the long, billowing dress, the one who had come to the door in her dream.

Chapter Six

Eddie did not have much to say, and neither did his friend. What had happened back at the theater was something they did not know how to talk about. But everything was different now.

He felt eyes on his back, watching from the parking lots and restaurants across the boulevard, from Fatburger's and the Weenie Wigwam and the cars parked there, and the cars that passed with windshields burnished by the sun over Reggae Rat's Cheesy Pizza Parlor; from the sidewalk before him and the trees along the curb, and the dirty leaves, and from behind the gnarled trunks, as if someone lay in wait, ready to snatch him up and drag him away and lock him in his room so that he might ponder the crimes he had committed but could not remember. All he knew was that someone who had trusted him now did not, and that left him hurt and angry and with nowhere to turn except inward, against himself. For reasons he did not yet understand, he was finally on his own.

They were only a few blocks from Tommy's house, but Eddie did not care if they ever got there.

"I'm sorry," he said.

"What for?"

"We could have stayed."

"Naw. *Ninja Cop* is a piece of shit."

"How do you know?"

"It was directed by Jim Wynorski."

"Well," said Eddie, "Robyn Harris is in it. Remember *Hard to Die*?"

"Yeah. But Joe Bob'll show it on *Drive-In Theater*. Just wait."

A candy-apple Dodge Capri drove by, top down, pumping out white rap. For no reason the teenaged driver flipped them the bird and shouted something obscene. The car passed, the shout dropping in tone like the sound of an ambulance receding. Eddie resisted the impulse to turn around and instead watched his shoes for a few steps, and the cracks in the cement, the stinkweed growing there, the gum wrappers and the silvered cellophane from the cigarette packages moored in the gutter, the detritus of the unplanned and decomposing landscape around them.

"Did you finish 'Scoops?" asked Tommy.

CALIFORNIA GOTHIC

Eddie had almost forgotten about *Cinema-Scoops*, the weekly column he wrote for the *Valley Sun*.

"Not yet." I'll write about *American Zombie II*, he thought. A summary of the plot, comparing and contrasting it with the original. That should be easy.

"And term papers are due Friday, don't forget."

"I didn't forget." Was Tommy on his case now, too?

"What's your topic?"

Eddie got a whiff of burning cheese and hot, oiled dough, and raised his head. The statue of Reggae Rat with its round, pizza-shaped mouse ears and black dreadlocks stood godlike against the sky across the street, its beady, polished eyes triangulated on the two boys. The sun's rays streamed around the huge plastic icon so that it seemed to rotate slowly on its axis, following their progress.

"Dario Argento," Eddie said.

"Miss Rippell approved *that*?"

"No. First I tried Carpenter. Then Romero. Then Cronenberg. But she didn't know who they are, either. So I'm calling it 'Horror Films.' It's still about Argento. She'll never notice the difference."

"You should have said Hitchcock. Everybody knows who he was."

"Boring."

"He had some good shots," said Tommy. "The staircase in *Vertigo* . . ."

"What about it?" They had watched the Criterion Collection edition, with the restored ending, just last week. Eddie held up his hands to form a square, sighting between his fingers at the remaining fast-food restaurants, as if seeing the street through a viewfinder. "A track-and-zoom. Like Spielberg, in *Jaws*. And about a hundred other people since then."

"Hitchcock invented it."

"Duh," said Eddie.

"I wonder what it would look like in reverse?"

"You mean track *forward* and zoom *backwards?*" It would flatten the perspective, thought Eddie. Or would it? He tried to imagine the shot.

"Somebody should do it," said Eddie.

"Maybe Jim Wynorski will."

"Or Charles Band."

"Or Fred Olen Ray," said Tommy.

"Or Anthony Hickox."

"Or Albert Pyun."

"Or Harley Cokliss!" Eddie cracked up.

"I'll try it," said Tommy, "on my dad's Hi-8."

"Can you get it?"

"Sure. He left it to me."

Eddie raised his hands again in the shape of a viewfinder and stepped in front of Tommy,

CALIFORNIA GOTHIC

sighting ahead. "Okay. We open on a tracking shot . . ."

"Hand-held," said Tommy.

"Panaglide," said Eddie, as his friend allowed him to be the cinematographer for this moment of their lives. Heat waves shimmered off the last of the cement as the sidewalk ended and the dirt began. Eddie panned in a half-circle, and saw the street as a set on a backlot, the cars entering and exiting El Pollo Muerto on cue, the customers at the tables outside merely extras gathered for a meal break. He whip-panned back to the dirt path and the lengthening shadows ahead. Then a Santa Ana breeze blew against his face and the mirage lifted, leaving only the flat, two-dimensional tones of the San Fernando Valley, bleached pastels left too long in the sun.

"Then?" asked Tommy.

"A montage. To set the scene."

"What scene?"

"The opening of *American Zombie III*."

Eddie's imagination was racing ahead, taking off from the disjointed movie they had just seen, in search of a thread strong enough to lead them through the maze of possibilities for yet another sequel. Why not? The implications of the story had yet to be realized.

"They haven't made it yet."

"They will."

"Who'd go see it?"

"We went to see this one, didn't we?"

"It'll go straight to video."

"Then we can see it real cheap," said Eddie. "Anyway, ours will be better."

"Maybe. What's the plot?"

"Well—" Eddie had to think. "First we see the bodies mutating . . ."

"Bodies?"

"Stacey and Shannon. The parts mutate and re-form. Into one person."

"Like the end of *Scanners*?"

"No," said Eddie, "not two bodies. One."

"They're both dead, right?"

"Right." Eddie replayed the last reel of *Zombie II* in his mind, the epic fight between the two women, so contrived and unconvincing. "But when they were fighting, they bit each other. So their DNA bonded. Now, when the pieces come back together, there's no way to tell who's who."

"Twice as smart, and twice as strong," said Tommy.

"And twice as dead."

"I like it. What's the location?"

Farther along the block, the street appeared to converge with the railroad tracks that ran behind the auto parts lot, parallel lines meeting at an infinite vanishing point. It was an optical illusion, but the tracks seemed to pass directly through the wrecking yard.

"There," said Eddie.

CALIFORNIA GOTHIC

"The Pick-A-Part?"

"Why not? That could be where the cars got taken after they blew up. Only what nobody knows is, there were pieces of Stacey in the wreck. And Shannon."

"Raul won't let us in."

"We could shoot after dark."

A twinkle like a mote of luminous dust appeared in Tommy's eye. "We couldn't do that."

"Couldn't we?"

"Have you ever been in there at night?"

"No," Eddie admitted. "Have you?"

"My dad caught me climbing the fence one time. He had a shit-fit."

There it is again, thought Eddie. *My dad*. The mention of Tommy's dead father made him want to change the subject fast. But his friend did not seem to mind. It was as if Mr. Oshidari were still alive. But he's not, thought Eddie.

"Why?"

"Raul has guard dogs."

"Oh. Then I guess the Pick-A-Part is out."

"Right. Your mother would have a shit-fit, too."

"I don't care," said Eddie, and meant it.

They came to the fence. The line of chain-links blipped by, steel diamonds joined to form a thick wire mesh. The links were reinforced with floppy strips of enameled aluminum, like a basket woven out of Levolor blinds; some of these strips had been bent or broken away by vandals or small animals trying to get in. Or out. Tommy took a Bic pen from his shirt pocket and ran it along the fence. The links vibrated and rang.

"If we bring our jackets," said Tommy, "we can climb in."

"How?"

"That's what they do in prison movies." Tommy indicated the razor-toothed coils atop the fence. "You throw your jacket over the barbed wire."

They saw a break between the galvanized steel pipes that supported the fence. It was still daylight so the long, rectangular gate was not latched but rolled back, wide open. A sign read:

PICK-A-PART

We Have What You Need!

There was no one inside, not even in the office trailer at the end of the dirt driveway. The office was hung with hundreds of old hubcaps that glinted dully, a collection of dented shields salvaged from fallen armies. Below the hubcaps, the desk was empty.

"Where's Raul?" said Eddie.

"Probably out back, taking a leak."

"What about the dogs?"

CALIFORNIA GOTHIC

"It's not dark yet."

Eddie started up the driveway.

"What time do you have to be home?" said Tommy.

Eddie briefly considered the clock in the office. It bore the picture of a girl who could have been Monique Gabrielle, the star of *Evil Toons*. SNAP-ON TOOLS, read the lettering around the face. The hands showed 5:30.

"Don't worry about it."

Behind the trailer, acres of wrecked cars were strewn across the lot, the twisted metal of a dishonored battlefield. Here, in what could serve as a burial ground for the internal combustion engine, rusty iron turned the earth the color of dried blood where it was not already black with motor oil. Hoods gaped, holding within their sprung jaws cracked blocks, air filters tipped like hats to reveal the smaller open mouths of carburetors. Tires rotted and liquefied among the weeds, ruptured sidewalls baring the unraveled sutures of frayed plies, brake cylinders leaked fluid into the tall grass, fenders lay like abandoned armor amid the dandelions. The smell of grease was everywhere, baked hard by the sun that now balanced on the uneven horizon, a corroding silver sphere suspended at the edge of a magician's torn handkerchief.

"This," said Tommy, "is where old Terminators go to die, right?"

Eddie had his hands up again in the shape of a square, going over the landscape one frame at a time.

He panned in short bursts, capturing a squashed Volkswagen piggybacked on a Cadillac, a mass of Detroit iron feeding on a Toyota, a Hyundai nipping at the soft radiator core of a Peterbilt. Exotic sports cars were as one with Buicks and Pontiacs, while Fords and Chevies faced off with broken but unblinking headlights and a Mercedes lay down with a Yugo. Near the fence at the back of the lot, something moved within the camper shell of a dysfunctional Datsun pickup. Eddie panned back and caught the shadow in his frame.

It was more than a shadow. A flash of white, and a man stood up in the back of the truck. He hitched his khakis over the crack in his buttocks, turned and spotted the two boys against the sea of drab machinery.

"Hey!"

The man climbed out of the truck and started toward them, his heavy body contained by the twin parentheses of his massive arms.

"Raul," whispered Tommy.

"I knew that."

"Hey! You kids want something?"

Before they had a chance to answer, there was another flash of white as a second figure sat up in the truck's bed. Her face was bisected by

CALIFORNIA GOTHIC

the edge of the cab, so that all they saw was a flicker of short hair like a dark flame on the air.

"We're just . . . looking," said Tommy.

"Well, if you don't want nothing," shouted Rafe, "get out!"

Behind him, the bisected face was watching them with a careful eye.

"It's okay," said a girl's voice. "They're friends of mine."

Who's she? wondered Eddie.

Raul kept coming. He was a tall, once-powerful Latino who had gone to fat, his neck still corded like a bull's and his thick arms matted with swirls of black hair. How AM I DRIVING? said his T-shirt. CALL 1-800-EAT SHIT.

The boys took several steps backwards, but then Raul veered off toward the office.

"Friends," he muttered, and spat.

"You know her?" asked Tommy, as soon as Raul was gone.

"I think I've seen her before," said Eddie.

"Lois Shaw," said Tommy slowly.

"The new girl?" He recalled the eighth-grade transfer student, the one who played flute in the school orchestra. "That's not her. That's—that's Eileen."

"Eileen *Larson*? No way!"

Tommy was right. But there was something familiar about the eyes, or at least the one they could see. It was catlike, round and clear and

135

with a lot of white showing, the kind of eye that watches you from the shadows in dreams.

"Then it's Sandy," said Eddie. "You know, the one in homeroom?"

"Maybe," said Tommy, unconvinced.

She could have been anyone, at least from this distance.

When she waved them closer, they walked forward as if through a minefield. For a moment she dropped from sight and Eddie wondered if she had really been there. Then they were at the truck and she rose up again, directly in front of them.

"Hi," she said.

"Hi." Which one of them said it? Eddie was not sure.

"I saw you before, walking."

"You did?"

"You're Edward, aren't you." It was a statement.

Edward? No one called him that except his mother, and Tommy's. But this time he did not mind the sound of it.

"Yes."

Now, at close range, Eddie decided she was not from the junior high. It was her voice that made him sure, as if she knew things that he had yet to learn. He could not make out her features; the sun had gone into the jagged horizon behind Reggae Rat's and she kept her chin

CALIFORNIA GOTHIC

down so that her hair hung over her forehead. But the voice was not shy, shaded with the promise of a deeper, more ambiguous meaning that was just beyond his grasp. Even her age was veiled and uncertain, like the girls Eddie had seen outside movie theaters and fast-food stands at night, girls who were always on their own with no curfew to keep, who grew up all at once and held that image for as long as they could until one day they were gone, moved away and never to be seen again, like the faces in clouds, before he had the chance to know them.

"What's your friend's name?"

"Tom."

"Hi, Tom."

"Hi."

"What are you . . . ?"

"What?" She looked at Eddie with amusement, as though he had started to make a joke.

"What are you doing here?"

"I was waiting."

"For what?"

"For you."

It was not true, of course. But Eddie liked the feeling it gave him: sweet and dangerous, like the smell of gasoline.

"Yeah, right," he said.

"Why are *you* here?"

"We're making a movie." Eddie wished he

could retrieve the words from the air. Now she really would laugh at them.

"What kind of movie?" she said, without blinking.

"Well, we're not making it *yet*," said Tommy.

"But you're going to," she said.

"Yeah."

"Where's your camera?"

"At home," said Eddie, unable to stop himself. "At his house, I mean. We're not going to shoot till tonight. When it gets dark."

"How can you do that?"

"The camera has a fast lens," said Tommy.

"Oh," she said. "I see."

Did she? Now it seemed to Eddie that she was making fools of them both.

"What are you really doing here?" he said.

She took a long time to answer. Eddie felt the weight of her silence like a force of nature.

"If I tell you," she said, "do you promise to keep it a secret?"

"Sure," said Tommy.

"I live here," she said. "Just for now. Raul lets me sleep in the truck. Until I move into my new house."

Eddie remembered something. "What time is it?" he asked.

"Quarter to six," Tommy said without looking at his watch.

"I gotta go."

CALIFORNIA GOTHIC

"Where?" she asked.
"I—have to meet somebody."
"Who? Your girlfriend?"
"No," he said too quickly. "Just a friend."
"I thought he was your friend."
Was she playing with him?
"He is."
"Am I your friend?"
"I don't even know your name," said Eddie.
"I'll tell you, tonight."
"Tonight?" said Tommy.
"When you come back to make your movie. I'll be your star."

Chapter Seven

As Evie drove away, Markham walked slowly through the empty house.

What was wrong?

She seemed all right now. And she would be back soon. Eddie had gone to his movie with the Oshidari boy . . .

But something was missing.

What?

Everything was the same as always, at least everything that showed: the sofa and chairs, molded to fit the shape of their bodies; the angle of light through the windows and the worn paths on the rugs and the shine and scuffs on the floorboards; the creaks and pops as the timbers of the house contracted in anticipation of the night; the air that moved from one room to the next, and the smells it carried, an invisible presence left behind by the life they had lived here, until the breath of their words and their laughter had been absorbed into the fabric of the curtains and the pores of the wood. Blindfolded, he could have identified this place.

The books were all here, a road map of their minds in the floor-to-ceiling shelves that made the walls appear thicker and more substantial. Separating the living room from the dining room was a basic library of science fiction, fantasy and mysteries, with history and politics in the hall, art and psychology in the den and film history, essays and humor confined to the spaces between. Rare first editions of novels, short story collections and poetry remained safely in the front bedroom, with cookbooks just outside the kitchen, and stacks of uncatalogable miscellany in the service porch. Countless boxes of dog-eared paperbacks, accumulated since college, had been banished long ago to the garage, to keep the mildew from spreading.

Eddie's room? It was decorated with movie posters, covering every square inch between the modular bookcases that sagged with video catalogues and ephemera, including the odd volumes he had taken from elsewhere in the house and not yet replaced. Some of the cases displayed plastic models, including one of Michael Myers, the avenging killer from *Halloween*, and a lucite holder containing an actual 35-mm. frame from *American Zombie*, originally offered as a premium to subscribers of *Shock Zone*.

CALIFORNIA GOTHIC

Markham had read the first few issues when they began arriving in the mailbox and found them surprisingly intelligent, able to analyze the best of the exploitation movies with a deep knowledge of cinema history. He would never have considered the relationship between Mario Bava and Martin Scorsese or Howard Hawks and John Carpenter, but now he knew otherwise, thanks to the insights of the remarkable Stefan J. He had even urged his son to try writing for the magazine, but with school there was no time. Maybe this summer, he thought, if Eddie did not spend every day of the week at the Cineplex or in front of the VCR. At least before we move and the world comes to an end, however temporarily.

Now the room was swathed in plastic sheeting from the roll Markham had found on the porch, so that everything—the bed, the desk, the tops of the bookcases—blurred beneath a transparent layer as if underwater. He remembered that he had to get the first coat of paint up before the boy came back. What time was it?

The tree was an unexpected wrinkle. Through the screen door he estimated the volume of wood he had cut. Even if he fired up the chain saw again and ripped through the logs one more time, there would be too much for the garbage cans, and the smaller, sharper pieces would tear holes in any trash bags.

He let the door swing shut behind him and contemplated the fruits of his labor. A mist of sawdust seemed to be suspended in the air, the fresh white particles still settling over everything in the yard, catching the rays of the afternoon sun like a covering of radioactive dust, while the rich, pungent aftertaste of tree sap lingered. No, he thought, if I cut it into bite-sized pieces I'll never get it all out of here.

There must be another way . . .

"Ow!"

The cry came from the remains of the tree trunk, which lay where he had dissected it, like the segments of a gigantic earthworm. Was someone—a child?—trapped under the fallen wood?

That was not possible.

Was it?

He lifted the branches but saw nothing, only hard, curled leaves and the bare earth beneath.

"Ow . . . !"

The sound was in the garage, he now realized.

He high-stepped over the chain saw and the discs of the trunk with their soft, pulpy cores exposed. The side door to the garage was ajar but he saw only blackness. Once inside, his eyes could not accommodate the sudden darkness.

"Eowww . . . !"

Gradually he made out the jumbled shapes of file boxes and loose planks of used lumber, a

CALIFORNIA GOTHIC

sheet of veneer, tarpaper and rolled asphalt, old paint cans and a generator, the convex eye of a broken television set on a flimsy metal cart; the picture tube was too thoroughly coated with dirt and grime to hold any reflection of Markham as he approached it.

Now, from below the rafters over the utility shelf, he heard a definite movement.

The stepladder was open against the shelf, where his son had placed it to get his box of magazines up under the old tarp. Eddie had done that, and then come out of the garage and gone on to meet Tommy.

Hadn't he?

Markham set his foot on the ladder.

Above, the cracked and brittle tarp rustled.

He climbed to the top and lifted it, and saw a pair of eyes staring back at him.

He stiffened, shifting his center of gravity. The ladder wobbled and began to give way beneath him.

The kitten poked its head out, ears flat.

"Oww!"

Markham tried to correct his balance. The ladder tipped, forcing his knees to lock. He flailed one hand, made contact with the shelf and clamped his fingers around the edge. When his knuckles clipped the kitten's nose it took a swipe at him and sprang. He felt needle claws digging into his scalp and then an almost weightless scurrying along his spine as the kitten leaped to the floor. Markham twisted to see where it landed, caught a glimpse of orange fur and a tail in the shape of an exclamation point rushing out of the garage. Then the ladder rocked, chattering away from the shelf. He managed to jump off an instant before it collapsed with a crash.

He landed on his feet and, despite a sharp jolt to the ankles, regained his bearings.

Damn cat, he thought, sucking the scratch on the back of his hand.

Now . . .

Where was I?

The wood.

What to do with it?

He paused, looking around the garage.

There were the sawhorses, the kitchen chair he had promised to repair, a case of motor oil, his toolbox. And, tucked away in the corner, what resembled a large wheelbarrow with high sides, mounted over a steel box.

The leaf shredder had not been used in years, since he had first dug out the original foliage and replanted. Would it still work?

He moved more junk, wheeled the device around the paint cans and out into the yard. The heavy-duty extension cord was coiled beneath a stack of old window screens. He con-

CALIFORNIA GOTHIC

nected the cord to the shredder, threw the switch and stepped back.

Nothing happened.

Was it jammed?

He started to reach over the steel sides and down into the hopper, but then he remembered the rotary blades.

He brought out the stepladder and positioned it so that he could see the mechanism.

There was a screwdriver at the bottom, its molded handle wedged between the cutters.

He got down long enough to disconnect the power cord. Then he climbed back up.

He almost got hold of the handle, but the edge of the hopper prevented him from leaning in all the way. He tried using a branch to knock it loose. After a few passes the screwdriver clattered into an upright position, its drop-forged shank pointing at his face like a missile ready to be launched. He leaned farther until his feet lost contact with the ladder, closed two fingers around the screwdriver and dragged it toward him with infinite care. Then he had it. He climbed down, reconnected the cord and threw the switch again.

When the blades began to whir, he tossed the branch in.

There was a thump, then a ripping as the blades tore through the wood. A cloud of white chips spewed out the side, falling like heavy snowflakes.

The yard needed mulching, anyway.

He added some twigs to the hopper. Instantly they were chewed up and regurgitated as detritus to conceal the dry ground under a blanket of fresh shavings. He added a double armload of leaves. The motor barely rose in pitch as the machine extruded confetti. He tested it with the big chunks. The motor screamed but tore through them, as well. He filled his arms and climbed the ladder again and again, allowing his eyes to close halfway as wood dust collected on his brow. Then there was only the whirring and the scent of the sawdust spackling his cheeks as so much deadweight was scattered to the winds.

"OWW!"

He wiped his face on his sleeve and glanced down.

The kitten had wandered over, curious. Now it arched and rubbed the ladder, its tail a striped question mark next to the chain saw and gas can.

"Get away," he said.

He could not even call it by name. They had yet to make the decision. Eddie wanted to call it Justin but Evie had vetoed that, at least for the time being. She wanted to see how it turned out first. It was only a few weeks old.

CALIFORNIA GOTHIC

A tentative paw touched the first rung.

"Go on, scat!"

That was what you were supposed to say to cats, wasn't it? But did they know what it meant?

Apparently not, because it continued climbing as the motor idled, settling into a steady hum.

Does he think it's purring? Markham wondered.

He had no more branches left to poke at the kitten. He extended one foot to block its passage, but it slipped sinuously around his ankle, caressing his shoe, and climbed higher.

Helpless, Markham observed its progress. When he tapped its pink nose with his heel, it embraced his foot and bit his shoelaces.

It would not take much longer to reach the top of the ladder.

He had to turn off the power. But the switch was too far away. He swung one leg out and tried to hook the cord. It was no use.

With one more rung unobstructed, the kitten pulled itself all the way up in a quick series of liquid motions. Then its paws dangled over the edge as it looked down into the hopper.

He bent over to scoop it up, but its fuzzy belly only slid over his hand as it wriggled higher. Now, its hind legs free of the top rung, it drew itself up onto the steel lip and balanced there, all four paws scrabbling for purchase.

In a flash he saw what was about to happen. The kitten attempting a leap across to the other edge, foreclaws desperate to hold the lip while its hind legs hung only inches from the idling blades. The tail would catch and it would be sucked down before it could make another sound, as a red rain began to fall . . .

"No!"

He threw himself over the open bin and turned to catch the cat in midflight. It writhed in his hands, a tiny heart ticking against his palm. He wrenched his body around, holding it high, and rolled off the machine. The ladder shot away from the side. He hit the ground on his back but his head struck part of the ladder with a ringing impact.

He did not know how long he lay there.

When he opened his eyes, his hand was throbbing. He released his grip and the kitten stopped biting his fingers. He saw it upside down, running away into the sky, as though the ground were overhead. When he tried to sit up, the yard began to spin. He lay back down next to the ladder and felt a hard knot of pain on the side of his head. He remained on his back, waiting for his vision to clear. But the view was grainy and he could not focus through the parti-

CALIFORNIA GOTHIC

cles, as if he were seeing the very atoms and molecules of the air colliding around him.

He raised himself onto one elbow and the scene inverted, the sky above and the yard below. It should have been familiar.

What is this place? he thought.

A garden.

He was transfixed by the patina of golden dust that lay between the house and the garage, a pathway paved with yellow bricks. The garden was alive as none he had ever seen before. The acacias and the palms might have been flocked with metallic paint, the spiderworts and bromeliads covered with ore from a dynamited vein in the motherlode. It looked like an enchanted grove in a storybook. Then there was a roar as a jet plane split the sky and disappeared behind a rock waterfall. The stones rumbled and leaves trembled, shaking loose more of the precious dust.

I wish Evie could see this, he thought.

If I try to tell her, will she believe me?

Then he thought, *Who is Evie?*

He forced himself to his feet, his head still ringing as the neurotransmitters in his brain switched on and off, overloaded by the rush of new information. There was an urgency about the ringing, as if a message of great importance were coming through on a direct line from God. Then the ringing relocated outside his skull, somewhere behind the screen door of the house. It seemed a purely arbitrary distinction.

When he brushed at his clothes, the gold dust began to tarnish. Sadly he turned away.

He went into the house and held the phone an inch from his ear, waiting for the message to organize into a meaningful pattern.

"Hello?" a voice was saying. "Is anybody there?"

"Hi," he said eventually.

"Hey, Dan."

"Hey, yourself." He knew the voice but could not place it.

"What's happening?"

Markham savored the extraordinary wit behind such a remark. "Everything," he said.

"That bad, huh?"

"That bad," Markham said, and felt his lips spreading in a wide grin.

"You told her, right? You poor schmuck. Well, how did it go?"

Whoever was on the other end was hilarious. "I'm not sure."

"Are you taking her to dinner?"

"I don't know yet."

"What about the movie?"

There was a clue. He seemed to remember someone who loved movies almost as much as he did, who was always ready to go to any revival house, anytime, on his say-so. She trusted

CALIFORNIA GOTHIC

his taste. The same with books. No, not books; that was the other one, later.

The other one?

"I have no idea what's playing," he said honestly. Truffaut? Bergman? Or the new Antonioni. That was supposed to be a good one. He had heard so much about it that he felt he had already seen it. "Maybe the one with Jack Nicholson."

"You're putting me on. *Terms of Endearment II*, or whatever the hell it's called? He hasn't made a decent flick since *The King of Marvin Gardens*."

Maybe so, thought Markham, but it hasn't been that long, has it? What's a couple of years? Give old Jack a break.

"Whatever," he said.

"What time are you leaving?"

"Not till . . ." His mind raced to put the name together. He wanted to be sure it was the right one. "Till she gets back."

"Well, the reason I ask is, Katie called me. She's already started on the Birdwell collection. I'm going over, but she says you'd better see it, too. There must be some primo material. Do you have an hour? Or should we put it off?"

"No."

"No you don't have time, or no you don't want to put it off?"

"How far is it?"

"The Stor-Ur-Self, remember? On San Fernando Road? You'll be back before she gets home."

There it was again. *She*. At least he knows. I need to talk to him, Markham thought. I have a lot of questions. "How are you getting there?"

The voice laughed. "Well, I could jump on my magic carpet, but I think I'll take the bug. At least it has a tape deck."

He does know, thought Markham. "Good. I mean, that's fine."

"Meet me there?"

"I don't know if I can drive," he said.

"Hey, are you okay?"

"I think so."

"That's cool—I'll pick you up."

How did I know he was going to say that? Markham wondered.

When they turned onto Laurel Canyon Boulevard, Markham began to understand.

The pieces fell into place against the brushed aluminum sky. It was late Saturday afternoon and business was bustling, the construction companies and furniture warehouses and lumberyards, with too many old Chevies and Fords caught now between trucks overloaded with heavy machinery. Beyond a chain link fence saw-toothed stacks of cinder blocks sparkled dully, like uncompleted pre-Columbian pyra-

CALIFORNIA GOTHIC

mids. A line of synchronized traffic lights converged in the distance as if indicating a landing path for incoming aircraft. He finally got it. There was nowhere else he could be but the San Fernando Valley, in no other time but the nineties; the overcrowding and decay had progressed just enough to bring him this far and no farther. The air inside the car was close and humid. He opened the passenger window as the painted fronts of fast-food stands flashed by outside Len's VW. It was not 1973, after all, or 1974 or 1975. A lot—all this—had happened since then. He was coming down.

"Are you really okay?" asked Len, grinding the stickshift back into second.

"I am now."

"She give you that bump on the head?"

Markham saw his wife's face scroll before his eyes, snapshot views of Evie in a summer dress with her hair tied back, then in an ankle-length coat, then in a fur-collared jacket—the ski lift at Big Bear? their honeymoon?—and then with her scoop-necked tank top and her legs tan and glistening from cocoa butter, the way she was now. She had not changed that much.

"I didn't tell her," he said.

"Good! You did right, my man."

Did I? he thought.

To gain further perspective, he concentrated on the closely packed suburban landscape in which he now found himself. Once, he remembered, the Valley had been a sleepy, sun-drenched place, an empty grid of long, narrow boulevards and neighborhoods connected by chalky new freeway extensions that ended at orange groves and dairy farms and breweries and factories, a place where there were as many escape routes from the densely-populated heart of the city as there were veins in your body; follow any one far enough and you would end up in a bedroom community with no traffic or gangs, where you could get a job and a house on a government loan and leave your car unlocked in the driveway all night, with plenty of space for the kind of desperate individualism that had brought so many here during the Great Depression; a place where you could start over on your own terms, reinvent yourself if necessary. But that was before the electric rail lines were dismantled and replaced by smoking buses and the tires and dirty fuel it took to run them, before the mergers and the bigger factories that sprang up along the way, until what had been isolated pockets of smog coalesced into a single cloud hanging over hundreds of square miles as if it were all one city, the freeways expanding like an octopus to draw everyone together, leaving no community untouched.

Now he wondered if the changes could be traced back to a single cause, a primal Big Bang

CALIFORNIA GOTHIC

that would account for so much devolution. Was what he saw simply one more stage of random growth, or was there a thread that had come loose somewhere along the line, unraveling the entire fabric?

He read the passing signs for a clue, but too many were written in languages he did not understand: Spanish, Japanese, Korean, Vietnamese, Thai, Tagalog. At some point something had changed, a detail too small for anyone to notice, like the introduction of a new charge into the atomic structure, one that alters and transmutes common substances, setting into motion a chain reaction that would eventually render every shape and surface unrecognizable, unless he could learn more about the alchemy. Or would he be useless to this new order whether he understood it or not?

"Remember *Bewitched*?" Len asked.

"The TV show?" said Markham. Elizabeth Montgomery, he thought, testing himself. "What about it?"

"Who was the guy?"

"What guy?"

"Samantha's old man."

"Why?"

"I was watching the Nostalgia Channel last night. I remember everybody else, but who played Darrin?"

It's trivia time, thought Markham. Okay, I'll

play. "Let's see. Aunt Clara and Uncle Arthur. Agnes Moorehead as Endora. And Serena, the evil twin. And the husband, Darrin. What was his name?"

Len ruminated, scratching his scraggly beard. "That's what I'm asking you."

"I got it. Dick York."

"No. He was on *Our Miss Brooks*."

"What did he look like?"

"Dark hair, the wet look. Medium tall. A crooked smile, like he was getting ready to cut a fart."

"That's him," said Markham.

"No, wait. I remember now. Dick Crenna."

"He was the guy on *Our Miss Brooks*. The goofy kid. Later he did that series about a senator, and some TV movies. Then he was in *Rambo*."

"Right, Dick Crenna," said Len.

"Dick York was in *Bewitched*."

"No way! Dick Crenna, and after a while he was replaced by another Dick. Sargent, I think. Look it up."

"I will."

For the next block or so, Markham almost believed him. What if it were true? A little thing like that. Dick York co-stars in *Our Miss Brooks*, Dick Crenna gets the part in *Bewitched*. He makes enough money, drops out, joins some church back East and dies of emphysema in the

CALIFORNIA GOTHIC

eighties. While Dick York goes on to play cops and senators and ends up as Stallone's boss.

Would it matter? Would everything be different today? Say there were these two butterflies back in the Cenozoic Age. One dies out, while the other one lives and reproduces. It would affect the food supply, the chemistry of the soil, the air, until we end up like this, with ideographs instead of English on every other sign, falafels and gyros and rice bowls and menudo instead of burgers and fries and hot dogs and Breakfast Jacks. And I'm stuck here in a place where nobody speaks my language and everything, the mores, the laws, the social behavior required to survive is entirely different, a world I don't figure in at all. Because something stupid, one single tiny detail, like Dick York and Dick Crenna switching roles on two TV shows, changes history. Would it? Markham lowered his head and avoided the window. It was just as well not to look too closely, at least for now.

"Five bucks says I'm right," said Len, settling into third gear.

Bucks, thought Markham. Male deer. Where did the expression come from?

"I believe you," he said.

"No, really. Check it out. In *Actors' TV Credits*, at the store."

"You're probably right." I hope to God you

aren't, he thought, squeezing his hands together between his knees until his fingers went white.

Len looked over at Markham, saw him hunched there. "Open the glove box."

"Why?"

"I picked up some new sides at Aron's."

Music, thought Markham. That's what we need.

"Like?"

"Take a look. I got Al and Zoot in there." Len leaned over and the glovebox dropped its jaw.

There were dozens of cassettes inside, with no room for anything else, not even a roadmap. A good thing they're not 8-tracks, thought Markham. What ever happened to 8-tracks, anyway? He spotted *Motoring Along*, a reissue of the old session with Al Cohn and Zoot Sims, featuring "My Funny Valentine" and "The Yardbird Suite" and "What the World Needs Now," as solid in his hand as a passport. Good to know that jazz was still around. He let out the breath he had been holding.

"Go on, play it. It's pretty tasty."

"On the way back," said Markham. Who were they going to see? Right, the girl who worked for them, the one with the freckles and the sunny smile. Reality locked in all the way. "How long has Katie been waiting?"

"A couple of hours. She only went because Birdwell's daughter keeps coming back, asking

CALIFORNIA GOTHIC

about the appraisal. I stuck around the store to close up."

The dashboard clock was broken, stopped at seven minutes past three. A.M. or P.M.? wondered Markham. At least it would be right twice a day. He checked his watch. It was later than he thought.

"When does the storage place close?"

"Six," Len told him.

"We won't make it."

"Sure, we will. We'll check it out and split. And send Katie home, so she can crash."

"At six o'clock?"

"She likes to take naps."

"You know that?"

"Not personally."

"Sure," said Markham.

"Really. She's got a thing for some guy."

And you've got a wife, he thought, remembering. "What guy?"

"I think he's a poet."

"Just what the world needs. Another poet." Ahead, a truck crept down a side road from the county landfill, its empty sides shuddering. "Don't sound so jealous."

"Me?"

"How's Jean, by the way?"

"Fine," Len said glumly. "I told her I'd be working late. She's got Evie to keep her company."

That's right, thought Markham. It's where my wife went. They would have plenty to talk about, as if they were Samantha and Serena, hatching secret plans behind their husbands' backs to make everything come out the way they wanted it. Whether Darrin was really Dick York or Dick Crenna. *Conjure Wife* as a sitcom. Why not? It was fiction, as real as anything else.

"Is he published?" Markham asked.

"Who?"

"Katie's poet."

"Now *you're* jealous."

"Just curious."

"I don't think so. If he was, we'd have to carry his book."

Markham saw two more trucks leave the landfill, huge banged-up Sanitation Department vehicles with hydraulic scoops jiggling on the roofs of the cabs.

"I bet he lives in Box City," said Len with a smirk.

"What's that?"

"Don't you read *Mother Jones*?"

"Not in a long time."

"They had an article. Box City was a commune up north."

"I didn't know there were any more communes."

"This one was some kind of mushroom cult. The Chief of Police in Santa Mara, he had a son

CALIFORNIA GOTHIC

who lived with them, at the city landfill. That's why they never got busted. Until now."

"Magic mushrooms?"

"What else? But it wasn't just the 'shrooms. Some kids got murdered in the town."

"Nobody ever killed anyone on psilocybin."

"True, but they split just the same. Nobody knows where they are now. The leader was that professor from the University of the Pacific, the one who wrote the guide to cultivation."

"The Fruiting Body?" No shit, he thought. The pseudonymous Dr. Barton Langstrom himself. "I used to stock it, when we first opened."

"Sell any?"

"Two boxes. Then the publisher went out of business—some post office drop in Berkeley—and we couldn't get any more."

Markham thought of another small publisher and his one and only book, *The Fire Inside and Other Poems.* Press On had gone out of business, too, before the book had a chance. Or so he told himself. He still had three cartons of the 750-copy print run in his garage.

They slowed to a crawl as the two trucks from the landfill moved into place ahead of them. Len pulled out to pass without bothering to signal. Markham heard the howl of brake shoes on worn drums and the bleat of a horn, so close that it might have been in the backseat. He jerked his head around in time to see a battered

Olds station wagon swerve to avoid bashing their VW from behind.

"Jesus, where did *he* come from?" Len yanked the wheel, but there was nowhere to go. The dump trucks were wheezing along on the right, bumper to bumper. The brakes on the Olds locked, trying to stop, and the big car began to weave as the driver fought to control it. Markham flung his arm over the seat and watched to see what would happen next.

"Punch it!" he shouted.

But too late. As Len tromped hard on the gas the transmission hesitated, then popped into gear with a groan and zipped the VW forward. The engine began to ping, a sound like BB's dropping into a coffee can. They slipped into line in front of the lead truck and slowed, keeping pace, as the Olds chugged by on the left. The other driver gave Len a deadly look. Next to the driver a woman crossed herself, clutching a string of black rosary beads. In the backseat, an indeterminate number of small children stared wonderingly through the fringe of swaying tassles that outlined the rear window. Markham was caught in the deep, tunnel-like gaze of a little girl with pierced ears and a lace collar. She sucked her fingers, calm as an Aztec princess on her way to the sacrifice, and would not let him go.

Ahead, the old Red Ball Moving and Storage

CALIFORNIA GOTHIC

building, now renamed Stor-Ur-Self, loomed above the skyline. It was no more than a block away, but at the pace the VW was able to move it might take them forever to close the distance. The building stood like a backlighted monolith against a constantly receding horizon.

"That bastard," said Len as the Olds finally passed.

"Take it easy. We're all right."

"How do you know we didn't get creamed back there?"

What was he talking about? It was close, but they had not made contact with the trucks, Markham was sure. As they turned the corner he saw the shadow of Len's wispy chin move like a ghostly silhouette across the dashboard, melting onto the dusty knee of Markham's trousers and up along his forearm, where it cast a small black shape like a tattoo of a spider on the back of his hand. The mesh of hairs settled back into place on Markham's arms, as he felt the adrenaline stop pumping and the throbbing in his kidneys subside. But the image of Len's bearded chin remained on his skin until they turned again and the interior of the car was thrown into shade. Markham glanced up and saw Len's knotted fingers flexing on the steering wheel as if he were still in street combat.

"We're clear, Lennie."

"Are we?"

"No, we're back between those two trucks, jammed up like an accordion, all right?" Markham saw through the trees to the next block and the back of the building. Len downshifted and came up behind it, staying close to the curb, his hands at ten and two on the wheel. "We're roadkill. The ambulance will be here any minute."

"Maybe."

They entered the lot through a gate in a chain-link fence and parked behind a pickup truck. He tugged on the handle and opened the door. Len got out slowly, his long legs unfolding grasshopper-fashion.

"Come on, Len. The war's over."

"Is it?"

They walked to the back entrance, a wide door built to accept pianos and oversized furniture, from a time when movers used the building to store unclaimed cargo. It had been converted for self-storage years ago but the door remained, conveniently functional. And there was still a loading bay to handle big rigs. Higher up on the bricks the weathered old Red Ball emblem showed through, and beneath that something else, perhaps the name of a livery company or a bottling factory, now only partially hidden under the faded, peeling layers. It was hard to tell which was the true underpainting and which were the forgeries.

CALIFORNIA GOTHIC

Standing in the shadow of the building, Len set his thumbs alongside his spine and adjusted his back.

"I guess it's just the Overlay."

"The what?"

"We're alive, sure—that's one possibility, like on a CD-ROM. You pick one and there you are. But then where are you? It's all possibilities. Theoretical scenarios. The trouble is, we can't *know*."

They went inside. There was a glass office with a desk, file cabinets and a fuse box with a mass of wires like dyed blood vessels sticking out of the top. Behind the glass a man made pencil notations on the classified section of a newspaper while eating a chimichanga.

"Birdwell," Markham said to him.

"She's already up there," the man said.

"I know."

"She just got here."

"A couple of hours ago, right?" said Len.

"Miss Birdwell?"

"McKenna."

The guard lifted a page on a clipboard. "Who?"

"There," said Markham. He put his finger on the sign-in sheet, pointing to Katie's signature.

"Oh, McKenna," said the guard. "She came at three-twelve."

"Right," said Len.

"So who are you?"

"The appraisers for the Birdwell estate," Markham told him.

"We spoke on the phone," said Len, "remember?"

"She's already here."

"I know," said Len testily. "So we'll sign in, too. We're here to help her. What's the number?"

"Six thirty-one."

Markham saw cement stairs in the far wall, leading up into darkness. "Where's the elevator?"

"Wait over there. I have to bring it down."

They vamped by an empty, brick-lined shaft while the guard hotwired the fuse box to bring the freight elevator back to the ground floor. Black, greasy cables hung down from the open vertical tunnel overhead, like dirty ropes dangling from a bell tower.

"So," said Markham, "you think we got killed back there?"

"No, I don't think that. I'm just saying, there are so many deaths, so many *possibilities* of death, that we can't know which one is really it. Not even after it's happened."

"Then it doesn't matter." *The Dead Are Alive*, Markham thought. *Sometimes They Come Back*. Nice titles. But the thought behind them made him uneasy.

CALIFORNIA GOTHIC

"Maybe," his friend said. "But then, maybe it does."

The cables jerked and a wooden platform descended. It came to a stop six inches above the floor.

"What do you think?" said Len. He belched and his expression lightened, the old playfulness returning. "Should I write it up and send it to *Omni?*"

"Sure," Markham told him. "As soon as you figure out a plot to go with it."

"Right, they always want that. The left-brained bastards. They can't leave off the training wheels. They need to keep it safe, so it's only a head game."

"I wouldn't know," said Markham. "I don't read science fiction anymore."

"Neither do I. They're full of shit. Like me."

They got on, closed the protective grating and punched the button for the sixth floor. The cables tightened and began to lift them up, past corridors of storage rooms with steel doors that wavered with the reflections of the electric light bulbs in the ceilings. The creaking of the overhead mechanism grew more strained as they neared the top of the shaft. Markham tipped his head back and saw Len looking up with him. The main cable was as dry as a petrified spinal column, with more than a few frayed strands. Metal particles fell from above and settled heavily around them, like iron shavings drawn to a magnet beneath their feet.

"I hope this thing doesn't break," said Markham.

"Maybe it did. We'll never know."

"That's funny. Real funny."

"Just one more piece of the Overlay," said Len, and winked.

They opened the grate and entered the maze of doors on the sixth floor, indistinguishable from each other except for the numbers. The rows of dented steel panels rippled and Markham thought of the tarnished silver mirrors in a funhouse, offset to create the illusion of choice while forcing the only possible route. Some of the doors bulged on their riveted hinges, as if battered repeatedly from the other side. But the only pounding to be heard was the sound of their footsteps.

"Six-nineteen, six-twenty-one . . ."

"Listen," said Markham.

Now faint music resounded through the hall. Markham saw a turn ahead, all but unnoticeable in the repetitive pattern of latches and padlocks. The doors they passed seemed to swell into the hall, throbbing like drumheads with the pulse of distorted bass notes.

"I know that rhythm section," said Len. "Where . . . ?"

"Up there. Around the corner."

CALIFORNIA GOTHIC

They turned at the next junction and the music was louder. One of the doors stood open, held back by a stack of encyclopedias.

"Here it is, six-three-one. Katie?"

Len knocked, as a tenor saxophone cut in with a powerful two-bar line.

He led the way into a twenty-by-twenty-foot storage room filled with close-packed rows of industrial bookshelves. The music was even more distorted inside, filtered through a cracked speaker. They stopped at the end of the first aisle.

"What the hell is that?"

"Steely Dan," said Markham. "Wayne Shorter. *Aja.*"

"Not that. *That.*"

Len meant the smear of paint on the wall. It was a symbol of some kind, a spot with crooked lines radiating out from the center. The paint was red and still wet, as if a huge bug had been smashed against the plaster.

"God damn gangs," said Len. "They get in everywhere."

"That's not gang writing."

"Then what is it?"

Markham counted the lines. "Eight legs," he said "Like a spider. I've seen this before . . . *Where's Katie?*"

Markham turned to the next aisle, where a row of shelves had tipped over. Books were dumped out into an insane pile, a first edition of *For Whom the Bell Tolls*, its dust jacket now ruined, and *Ulysses* and *The Grapes of Wrath*, *The Outsider and Others*, *Without Sorcery*, *Dark Carnival* and *Now Wait for Last Year* tossed down together like kindling for a bonfire. A boom box was half-buried at the edge of the pile, still blaring music from its cracked housing. Markham nudged it with one foot; the batteries fell out and the music stopped. Then he saw that the radio lay in a puddle the same color as the smear on the wall. The puddle was spreading.

He tore through the pile, flinging aside copies of Updike and Bellow and Pynchon, Faulkner and Bukowski and Patchen, Salinger and Sterne and King, all fallen together as if about to be pulped. A vellum set of Fielding soaked up some of the liquid on the floor, a sticky trail that led to a freckled hand that was still warm.

Katie's matted hair was now bright red, as if washed in henna. She lay where she had fallen, pinned to the floor like a monarch butterfly with its wings broken.

"The books!" Len said, cradling her in his arms. He smoothed the hair away from her forehead. "The fucking books . . . !"

Her eyes were open, and so was her throat, from the windpipe to the carotid artery.

Markham slumped against the wall for support. His hands came away sticky. They were red, too, as red as the blood that had been used like fingerpaint on the wall.

"It wasn't the books," he said, as far away down the hall the elevator mechanism began to grind and squeal. He looked more closely at the blot.

"Then what?" cried Len. *"What?"*

"A tarantula," he said, too softly for Len to hear. But that was what it was. An eight-legged emblem that had once belonged to the CSA, a cult that no longer existed.

Chapter Eight

The way the red lights shone, Evie thought the sun had not yet set but was only now going down behind the building, penetrating the bricks and mortar with beams of fire. Then she saw the police cars wedged in front of the entrance, bubble machines flashing, and quickened her pace. She wanted to appear calm but she must have crossed the distance at close to a run, because by the time she got there Jean was far behind, somewhere back by the parking lot fence and unable to catch up.

Dan was inside, sitting next to Lennie in the office, as they repeated their story to the officer in charge. She tapped on the glass to catch his eye. He glanced up and acknowledged her with a nod and an expression so neutral it chilled her to the bone. Then he stopped talking and stood, his brow furrowing as his mouth simulated a

DENNIS ETCHISON

smile. He said something to the officer and came out to meet her.

She held him, rubbing the back of his head. "Are you okay?"

She felt him nod against her neck.

"We got here as fast as we could. How's Katie?"

He pulled away and shook his head. He looked past her as Jean entered the building.

"All right, what's going on?" Jean demanded. The officers ignored her. She raised her voice. *"Where's my husband?"*

Lennie came out and held her hand.

"Take it easy," he said. "They're about finished with us."

"What the hell is this about?" said Jean. She was breathing heavily and her eyes protruded starkly from their sockets. "You didn't tell me jack shit on the phone!"

Lennie put a finger to his lips. "It's cool," he said. "They just want to ask us a few questions."

"Did something happen to your little whore?"

"For Christ's sake, Jeannie!" The officers stopped talking and he forced a laugh. "Katie had an accident. She's *dead*, all right?"

Evie turned back to Dan, his face only inches from hers.

"Is it true?"

He did not answer.

She saw the fine lines around his eyes and the

CALIFORNIA GOTHIC

white hairs mixed in with the brown ones on his head, more than she remembered. He was looking nervously past her, through the wide doorway to the parking lot outside.

Oh God, she thought, I don't know if I can deal with this. I don't want to know. Not yet. Later. It's too much.

"You must be so tired," she said. "Let me take you home."

"Is Eddie here?" he asked.

She could see by the pain in his eyes that the question mattered to him. He was a good father. Evie did not have the heart to disappoint him and so sought for a way to put it that would sound right, what he needed to hear.

Before she could answer the guard passed them on the way to the glass office, accompanied by one of the policemen. "I told you before," the guard was saying. "She signed in. It's on the board."

"You sure it was a she?" said the policeman.

"I saw her! Everybody has to sign their name and the time."

"What did she look like?" Dan asked him.

"Young, kinda pretty. Like one of those—"

"I mean the other one," said Dan. "The second one."

"That's what I'm telling you! Miss Bird-something. You know her, right?"

"No," Dan said, loudly enough to be heard by everyone. "I didn't know her."

"She must have gone up before us," said Lennie. "The freight elevator was already at the top, and he had to bring it back down. So—"

"Somebody could have taken the stairs, couldn't they?" said the officer.

"The elevator wasn't there," said Dan, "when we came out of the room. So somebody had already taken it down."

"And you didn't pass anyone in the hall?"

"There are a lot of halls up there. So she obviously found another route."

"Are *you* sure it was a she?" the officer said.

"That's what *you* said." Dan held the guard's arm long enough to turn him around. "You saw her. Didn't you?"

"Miss Birdwell," said the guard. "Not the first one. The second one."

"There was only one Birdwell," said Lennie. "The first one's name was Katie McKenna. M-C-K . . ."

"And you didn't see anyone come down on the elevator," the officer said to the guard. "Were you in the office?"

"Damn right I was!" said the guard. "I work till six, and I do my job good. Can't nobody say I don't!"

"Maybe he was in the head," said Len.

"No way!"

CALIFORNIA GOTHIC

"We'll ask the questions," said the officer.

"I hope you're finished with my husband," said Jean. "Because I've been on my feet all day. He doesn't know anything. If you don't need him . . ."

"Take a seat," said the officer.

"Where? I don't see any more chairs around here! Lennie, I'll bring the car around and we'll all go get a drink. Right, Eve?"

"Well, I . . ."

"What did she look like?" Dan followed the guard, dogging him for an answer.

Evie was left standing alone on the cement floor. It was so cold there were cracks in it like the ice on a frozen river. She felt it chilling the bottoms of her feet through the thin rubber soles of her shoes. She heard a clanging behind her and tensed her shoulders, as the cables tightened in the open elevator shaft.

"Like a college girl or something, all right?" the guard was saying.

The elevator platform descended, carrying a wheeled gurney and several men in leather-soled shoes. There was a heavy plastic trash bag on the gurney, with a zipper running from top to bottom. A body bag, she realized. The zipper was closed. Her eyes teared up and she turned away. Somewhere a siren wailed.

Dan said to Lennie, "Then it wasn't Birdwell." They were trying to keep their voices down but

Evie heard their whispers clearly, like the rustling of leaves on marble.

"Could have been," said Lennie.

"You've met Birdwell," said Dan.

"Yeah."

"She's not young."

"She looked young to me."

"When?"

"At the store. She came in twice today. She talked to Katie."

"About what?"

"Well, she wanted to know where you were. Katie said she was meeting us here. She got the address . . ."

"What did she need the address for, if this was her father's storage? She'd know it."

"Maybe she forgot."

"Lennie, I met Birdwell's daughter a month ago. She was in her forties—her *forties*, Len. Not some college girl."

"Then if it wasn't Birdwell," said Lennie, "who was it?"

The siren rose and fell, coming closer. An ambulance arrived behind the police cars. Dan left Lennie and went to the door. He stood there, sweeping the parking lot with his eyes as if searching for something, as the sky darkened beyond the spinning red lights.

Evie came up next to him. She put her arms around his waist and rested her head on his

CALIFORNIA GOTHIC

shoulder. But his arm muscles became taut, as if shooing away a fly that had landed there.

"I asked you a question," he said to her.

It was up to her to be strong now. "Honey, let's go home, okay?"

"Cut it, will you?" he said fiercely. "Just answer me. *Where's Eddie?*"

"I don't know," she said. "I left him a note . . ."

And then the fear returned, and this time there was no stopping it.

Chapter Nine

Tommy went for the camera, and Eddie started home. He walked out of the wrecking yard and alongside the fence till he came to the intersection and the tracks. Teenagers on dates passed him in cars, and families heading home from early dinners at Carrow's or Marie Callender's or Two Dollar Bill's. He realized that he was hungry; there had been no time for food at the Cineplex, and on the way back from the mall neither boy had thought of eating. But now, imagining a meal out with his parents, maybe a pizza, not even delivered so that he could tear off a slice and take it to his room, his appetite left him.

He pictured himself going into the house, where his mother and father would be waiting while pretending they were not, as passive as the hippies in *The Trip* or *Psych-Out*, too mellow to say what they were really thinking. He would rather his dad yelled at him right off, instead of turning away as if there was always something wrong with his face or clothes or the way he combed his hair, as if they expected him to run into the furniture or knock a hole in the wall with his big, clumsy feet.

It was his mother's fault.

He remembered his dad, the way he was years ago, always joking around, with a funny answer for her whenever she got depressed and took it out on them. Something had happened to his father; the fun had gone out of him so that he lost his nerve to stand up to her. And it was getting worse. He saw his father's face before him, pale, washed-out, the bags under his eyes and the lines in his forehead getting deeper all the time, as though he were aging in some lap-dissolve process shot that would end with his cheeks sucking in and the skin crumbling off his skull. If I don't watch it, Eddie thought, the same thing will happen to me.

Now, with the sun down, he was in what cameramen call the Magic Hour, when shadows are full of half-tones and background and foreground are no longer clearly separated, the edges of objects defined by thin luminous lines, like a television screen when the Sharpness control is turned up all the way, and the entire scene overlaid with an electrified platinum wash. As he crossed the tracks the rails blended with the ties and gravel, disappearing into the flat, grainy depths between the boulevard and the residential section beyond. He could not decide whether to keep going. He felt a tingling and stopped, one foot on the tracks, expecting the vibration of a train from miles away in the darkness ahead. Then he saw the foxtails growing next to the spikes and remembered that the rails were no longer in use. The tingling was not really in his tennis shoe but in his bones. It was a signal that something was coming, not from far away but inside himself, and it felt like a moment between the end of spring and the start of summer, like a promise and a warning carried together on the Santa Ana wind, like the light. He could not refuse it. He crossed the tracks and walked on.

The windows were dark, as if his was the only uninhabited house on Stewart Way. Others shone with cheerful activity behind open drapes; kitchen blenders hummed as dining room tables were set, while living room TV's sang with commercials and news reports. Only his home appeared to be abandoned. In the deepening twilight the lawn might have been unmowed, the porch blown full of leaves from every tree on the street.

His mother's car was here. Then why weren't the lights on? Was she sleeping already, buried under the covers in one of her extended weekend naps?

Or was she waiting for him in the darkness, with more questions?

He listened by the front bedroom for a sound from inside, but it was no use. The evening news was too loud, as if magnified through a tunnel, every TV set on the block relaying the same announcer's voice from house to house:

". . . *Police suspect arson. The bodies of two people in the cabin were burned beyond recognition . . .*"

He cut along the side to the backyard. If the rear door was unlocked, that meant Mom was here. There was one way to find out. He put his hand on the knob and was about to twist it when he heard, no felt, no *sensed* something rushing toward him.

He turned around.

No one was there.

That did not surprise him. He hadn't expected to see anyone there, not exactly. But *something* . . .

What he saw was not a presence but an absence. Part of the yard was missing. The bushes were there but now a darkness was open in the center, a gap that ran all the way to the fence. The shrubs around the gap were bending, as though under the weight of the curved light that outlined their leaves. As he stared into the empty space, the branches moved.

The wind entered the yard like an invisible intruder, climbing over the fence and heading for the back door, shaking loose the dirt that had collected on the weeds and plants. The wind blew something into his face. He blinked and dug a particle out of the corner of his eye, then rubbed his fingers together. It was sawdust.

He opened the back door, reached in to turn on the service porch light, and looked again.

Where was the tree?

He had swung from it as a child, climbed it as a boy, but now it was gone. In its place was an empty spot that made the yard look even uglier. Had she forced Dad to cut it down? He saw the chain saw on the ground and the old leaf-shredder near the garage, and knew that he would never play here again.

He did not want to go any farther than the kitchen in case she was home. He hesitated by the refrigerator, then pulled on the door. A leftover tuna casserole, a loaf of raisin bread, low-fat milk, jack cheese . . . He grabbed the cheese and what was left of a one-pound chocolate bar from Trader Joe's and started for the table, then decided not to wait around. He stuffed the cheese and chocolate into his jacket pocket. I'll leave a note, he thought. There was the magnetic tablet on the refrigerator door, but where was the pencil? It was never here when he needed it.

He went to the hall without turning on the light.

The house was as silent as a tomb. It was hard to believe, but she had forgotten to lock up, even though she always made such a point of it with him. They had taken Dad's car and not waited around to see if he was coming home. I said I would, Eddie thought. She doesn't believe me anymore. What time is it, anyway? Seven? Not that late. She could have waited. In case I wanted to go with them. Which I don't.

In the hall, he heard what sounded like a bird.

How did it get inside? The screens were still in place on the windows . . .

The flapping seemed to be coming from his room.

He felt a shudder as he pushed the door open.

Everything—the bed, the bookshelves, the desk and computer—was covered with plastic, like floor samples in a department store. The window was up a few inches the way he had left it and a breeze now blew in with enough force to move the dropcloth in long, snapping waves.

The anger came then. Dad had said he would paint the room—Mom's idea. He hadn't done it yet but she had made him leave it this way just the same.

CALIFORNIA GOTHIC

So where am I supposed to sleep? Under *this*? No way!

He lifted it long enough to stick his hand into the desk drawer for a pencil.

Then he slammed the door, stomped to the kitchen, scrawled a note and left.

What if I wanted to work on my column tonight? What was I supposed to do? Go to the library?

Does anybody care that I live here anymore?

In the junkyard, something stirred.

"Tommy?"

The only answer was a slight movement in the weeds, as if something buried were returning slowly to life, like in *The Plague of the Zombies*. But it was not quite ready to show itself.

He panned from side to side.

To his left the gutted chassis of a Buick Regal creaked, cooling as night fell; to his right, a line of engine blocks seemed to inch forward like the derailed components of a skeletal train, plowing to a slow-motion halt in the protracted twilight. Directly ahead was an empty half-acre that had not yet been filled, an open meadow covered by uncut grass.

"Is anybody here?"

He felt the weight of heavy machinery behind him, and a shimmering heat as the junked iron and steel radiated the last of the day's warmth. He turned quickly, but the close-packed cars had not moved. The wind had come with him to the lot, carrying exhaust fumes from beyond the fence, as if the city were exhaling the poisons of the day. The layers of air blew across the basin, leaving a transparent undertow to pour through the gate, where it would be reheated one last time by the wrecked cars before night fell. The wind blew over Eddie and parted the weeds before him like an unseen river winding toward a hidden shore.

The weeds in the distance began to wave, too, a long gap that started from the opposite direction, by the fence at the far side of the lot. The gap deepened, became a path, an aisle opening between the cars stacked on either side, then split into two parallel black lines.

Now the grass fell more quickly as the lines closed the distance, aiming straight for him.

Then he heard the growling.

He stepped aside but the lines swerved, homing in. He flattened his body against the door of a Peterbilt. The lines turned like torpedoes through sea grass. He tried holding his breath but his asthma chose this moment to return. His throat closed and he began to wheeze.

Where was Raul? He could call off the dogs. He would, any second now.

Eddie climbed up onto the running board and

CALIFORNIA GOTHIC

tried to open the cab. The door was stuck. He yanked it, rattling the dented sheet metal, but that only made more noise. The dogs would hear. They would know.

He struck the driver's window with his fist. His hand was too soft. He felt the knuckles bruising and his face swelling as his eyes closed tighter and his balance faltered. His chest burned and his lungs hurt as if impaled on his ribs.

He clasped both hands together and brought them down like double axe-handles.

The windshield went white as the safety glass fractured but did not yield. Then he heard the slobbering and the snapping of teeth as the first dog leaped at the truck.

Tweet.

A whistle cut through the air.

The two dogs dropped back into the grass, watching him with murderous eyes.

"Eddie . . . !"

Tommy's voice.

Then there was the hollow sound of rubber soles thumping on hard-packed earth, and laughter.

"Hey, Ed, what are you doing up there?"

Eddie looked down from his perch and saw Tommy standing by the truck. His friend had a peculiar grin on his face.

"What are *you* doing down *there*? Watch out . . . !"

The guard dogs sat trembling on their haunches, ready to attack. Tommy's arms hung loosely at his sides, as if he did not care about his fingers, the camera bag slung casually over one shoulder.

Someone else came up next to him.

She reached down to pat one of the muscled napes. Then she and Tommy looked up like an amused couple.

Eddie forced himself to breathe as he lowered his foot to the black ground.

"Who whistled?"

"I did," said the girl.

She stopped stroking the dog's lathered coat. The neckline of her loose dress fell open in the near-darkness. Then she stood straight again, taller than Tommy by at least two inches. Tommy didn't seem to mind.

"Oh," said Eddie. "I thought it was Raul."

"He went home," said Tommy, and smirked. In the gray light his lips opened unevenly, exposing wet silver-and-plastic braces, and closed as he savored the words. "For the rest of the night."

"How did you do that?" Eddie said to the girl.

"Do what?"

"Get them to stop."

"Easy," she said. "I just whistled."

CALIFORNIA GOTHIC

"Yeah," said Tommy with a grin. "You know how to whistle, don't you? You just put your lips together, and blow!"

Eddie stood where he was, watching the two of them standing so close together. The girl squatted down again, and her knees moved up to her chest and popped out from under the hem of her dress like two more tight breasts. She put her mouth close to the dogs' ears and whispered something.

Then she said, "Give me your hand."

Which one of them did she mean? The boys extended their arms. She took a hand from each in her long, cool fingers and drew them close to the dogs' noses. Eddie felt their hot breath condensing on the hairs of his wrist. Then the dogs ran off.

"Now you're safe," she said.

"How do you know?" asked Eddie.

"They have your scent."

"So?"

"They only kill strangers."

She forgot to let go of Eddie's hand. Her skin was not what he expected. It was firm on the palm, soft on the back.

Tommy unshouldered his bag and lifted out the Hi-8 camera. He handed it to Eddie.

"Here, take a shot of us, okay? It's just that little button there."

The camera. The movie. Why had they ever

mentioned it to her? It was a game, a kind of joke between them, something to pass the time, nothing more. But now they were locked into it, because of her. Of course they couldn't make a real movie . . . though if they came up with a plot for *American Zombie III* it was possible that they could sell it to the company that had made the first two. Or was Eddie still thinking like a child? The notion hung like a question mark in the air between them, and whether it was the last stubborn trace of childhood or something larger, more substantial, the promise of a future that cast its shadow backwards through time, ready to be seized, Eddie could not know.

What he did know was that Tommy was not asking him to shoot a horror movie now. His friend wanted a record of the girl and himself with her. It would not become a true memory unless it could be replayed over and over again, as many times as it might take to make it real.

Eddie took the camera and raised it to his eye.

He saw only Tommy in the frame.

Where was she?

Tommy's crooked grin fell closed over his shiny teeth and gums.

"Hey, where . . . ?"

Neither boy finished the sentence.

"Over here," she said.

"Where?"

CALIFORNIA GOTHIC

"Here."

Now she was at the end of the truck. How had she moved so fast?

"Please?" said Tommy. "It's just a test . . ."

"First you have to catch me."

Eddie detected a blur by the Peterbilt, a charcoal figure smudging. Again he raised the camera and adjusted the eyepiece. Then Tommy disappeared around the cab and the frame was gray and empty.

"I'll get her!" Tommy said too loudly, his voice strangely hoarse, and was gone.

Eddie started around the Peterbilt, then heard the patter of feet running away.

He walked the length of the big rig with the camera to his eye, expecting to find her at the other end, but when he got there he did not even see Tommy.

There were many places where she could hide. It was too dark to see into the other cars. Bits of glass hung suspended in broken windshields like smashed spiderwebs, fenders wavered, chrome bumpers melted. Eddie locked the RECORD button, sure that none of this would register on tape except for the tiny streak that seemed to be following him. It was the reflected image of his lens moving along the line of cars, reflecting in turn the illuminated icon of Reggae Rat that rose into the sky farther down the block, beyond the boundaries of the lot.

Open on an abstract pattern, he thought, unable to control his imagination. *Moving across the random shapes of a junkyard at night . . .*

EXTERIOR NIGHT - JUNKYARD - HAND-HELD (PANAGLIDE)

Shadows inside cars. Cushions splitting open to show sharp, rusty springs. Steering wheels at odd angles. Backseats so dark they might hide anything. But the cars are all empty, as far as we can see. . . .

Eddie stepped over a flaking brake drum and continued to the next row.

ANGLE DOWN into one car, to be sure there is no one inside.

SOUND: a *scratching*.

PANNING around quickly . . .

To see only more wrecks.

CLOSING IN on one of the wrecks—to show:

A *movement*.

CALIFORNIA GOTHIC

In the flatbed of a pickup truck. But what? A gas can, a sleeping bag, a Coleman chest . . .

The top of the chest is open.

Something is inside.

Closer . . .

To see a RAT nibbling away at some spoiled food. Has someone been living in the truck?

If so, they are gone now. Or are they?

The sleeping bag is lumpy, as if concealing a *long shape*.

Is it a body?

A HAND reaches from behind camera and opens the sleeping bag, to reveal:

A *rotting face!* Eyeballs hanging out, the flesh decomposing over a gaping skull!

Eddie lowered the camera.
There was no skull, no body. A Coleman chest

and some blankets. No rat. But somebody had been sleeping here.

I found her lair, he thought. The place where she returns each night, to feed. Does she sleep? No, of course not. She's a zombie, remember?

Then whose truck is this? It's not wrecked like the others.

The nightwatchman. That's it. We'll call him Raul. She found him, and fed. Now she knows everything he knew about this place. For a while she will make it her world. Until she's ready to go out and seek her revenge . . .

He returned to the viewfinder.

>**REPORTER (OFFSCREEN)**
>Oh my God!

>**CAMERAMAN (O.S.)**
>Keep rolling.

>**REPORTER**
>(clearing his throat)
>We've just made a grisly
>discovery. The body of—
>of a—

>**CAMERAMAN**
>Where's Bob? Tell him to go
>back to the van and call the
>police. . . .

CALIFORNIA GOTHIC

REPORTER
I don't *believe* this!
We come here to shoot a
follow-up . . .

CAMERAMAN
Keep rolling. This is an
exclusive.

REPORTER
Jesus, Joseph and Mary,
what *is* that?

CAMERAMAN
Just some derelict. Start
again, before the cops
get here. "All that's left
of the Olympia empire after
the conflagration earlier
tonight," etc. Do the
lead-in, so we'll have it on
tape. We can fill back at
the studio.

REPORTER
I can't. The smell.

CAMERAMAN
Where the hell is Bob?
I'll make the call—Jerry,

take over. I'll meet you
at the gate. Set up wide,
so we get the cops arriving.

The camera shakes as it changes hands.

The REPORTER staggers into frame
and retches.

>   **REPORTER**
> Cut, for God's sake.
> I'm sick.

>   **CAMERAMAN**
> Wait a minute. What the
> hell is *that?*

Behind the reporter, there is a movement from the far side of the truck.

>   **REPORTER**
> A body. You've seen
> dead bodies before.

ZOOMING IN on a *white blur*. Elusive.

>   **CAMERAMAN**
> Not that. *There.* Don't
> you see it?

CALIFORNIA GOTHIC

> **REPORTER**
> Maybe you can find something artistic about it. Me, I'm going to find some Alka-Seltzer.

WHIP-PAN along the truck . . .

Centering on a *flash of white*.

> **CAMERAMAN**
> Lights!

The **PORTABLE LIGHTS** follow, to catch:

A **GIRL**'s face.

She freezes like a young deer caught in headlights. But she is calm. Unafraid.

> **CAMERAMAN**
> Uh, hi there. Can you talk to us for a minute? We're from Eyeball News.

Now she walks forward, away from the wreckage—and we see that she is completely *nude*.

WHIP-PAN over to the REPORTER. He is watching wide-eyed.

> **REPORTER**
> I hate to tell you, boys,
> but we can't use this.

> **CAMERAMAN**
> Maybe *you* can't! I'm rolling!
> Go!

The REPORTER shrugs and plays along.

> **REPORTER**
> Name, please?

The GIRL is beautiful. Like a centerfold. She has an even, golden tan. But she is not smiling. Now her eyes focus purposefully.

> **GIRL**
> Stacey.

> **REPORTER**
> Spell it? For the record.

> **GIRL**
> S-h-a-n-n-o-n.

CALIFORNIA GOTHIC

> **REPORTER**
> You mean that's your
> last name?

He comes closer to her, holding out the microphone.

> **GIRL**
> No.

> **REPORTER**
> Well, which is it?

> **GIRL**
> Both. The last name is
> Marston.

> **REPORTER**
> You mean Marston of
> Olympia Chemical? The *late*
> Robert Marston. Are you
> related to . . . ?

> **GIRL**
> You might say that. I'm
> in charge now.

She reaches out as if to take the microphone—but grabs the reporter's wrist instead.

She pulls him toward her, with such force that he is yanked off-balance and falls into her arms. For a moment she holds his face against her breasts. Then she wraps her arms around his head and squeezes.

SOUND of his *neck breaking*.

Before he can fall, she lifts him off his feet and hurls him away. His body sails through the air and lands on top of the truck, where it lies twisted and lifeless.

Then she looks into the camera lens. Approaching. Her face filling the frame.

> **GIRL**
> You want a statement?
> I'll give you one.
>
> **CAMERAMAN**
> Th-that's all right. Jerry!
> Bob! Cut! Excuse me, but if
> it's all the same to you, I'll
> just fast-forward my ass out
> of here . . .

CAMERA turns sideways as he sets it down. Still recording.

CALIFORNIA GOTHIC

At the edge of the tilted frame, we see her grab the CAMERAMAN by the hair as he tries to run. She pulls his head back . . . leans over him from behind . . . and kisses him deeply on the lips, as if sucking something from him.

He groans and struggles but she won't let go. She bends his head back farther, holding it by the hair . . . until his *spine snaps*.

Then at last she breaks the kiss, still pulling . . . and *tears his head from his body*.

His neck spurts hot blood.

She holds the head high in one hand as she licks her lips. Tasting.

Then she drops the head into the grass like a discarded apple. She steps over the camera . . .

And is gone.

Yes!
Eddie tore his face away from the camera and

looked up. He knew he had it, the opening sequence of *American Zombie III*.

There was no way for him to shoot effects like that.

Then what were they doing? Still playing? Like kids?

But we're not kids anymore, he told himself.

He thought, I'll write it myself, as a screenplay. Who knows? It's worth a shot.

He had no idea what would happen next. But it was a start. For now, it was all in his head.

Wasn't it?

Then why did he still see the blur of golden-white skin in front of him?

It was there, at the end of the truck, beyond the ruined radiator.

"Hi," he said. "Where's Tommy?"

She did not answer. What was her name? She hadn't told them that yet. It was part of the secret they would have to discover, who she really was, what she was doing here. And what she wanted from them. She was older; why would she want *anything* from them?

Maybe she really wants us to take her picture, he thought.

Or she's putting us on. One big joke.

It was time to find out.

"Well, do you want to be in this movie or not?"

CALIFORNIA GOTHIC

Now she walks forward, away from the wreckage . . . nude.

Not much chance of that. But he could not stop imagining what her body would look like.

In the shadows, the blip of white gold went out.

All right, he thought, if you want to play . . .

He cut between the rows as flickers of light shot through the wrecks from the perimeter of the lot. As he picked up speed so did the lights, strobing faster. Wind whistled under punctured oilpans and in the jaws of open hoods. It sounded like laughter, taunting him. He dropped to his knees and tried to spot her ankles running in the next row but the weeds were high and dark, as if earth and machinery had grown together to form a landscape where the dividing line between organic and inorganic, between the living and the dead no longer existed. He got to his feet.

Now, at the end of the row, there was a yellow glow, a circle of light swelling in the distance.

What was it? *Where* was it?

He saw that he was standing again by the Peterbilt. He had come back to the place where he started.

"Tom-my!"

He touched his lips. They were parted as the wind blew across his open mouth, but it was not his voice.

He climbed a stack of fenders nested like spoons, and saw the office trailer with the lights still on inside. There was a small stick-figure near the gate. The figure put its hands to its mouth and called again.

"Tom, damn you! Come on out!"

It was Mike, Tommy's older brother. He was standing just inside the grounds, his letterman's jacket tinged with light from the trailer. Outside the gate, his Explorer was parked at the curb.

Eddie ducked and started to climb back down, but too late.

"Tommy? That you?"

Walking to meet him, Eddie hid his face behind the camera.

EXT. NIGHT - ENTRANCE TO WRECKING YARD

A YOUNG COP cruises by, spots the open gate, and parks his squad car. He enters the grounds, sees the NEWSVAN . . .

As Jerry, the DRIVER, hurries up.

    DRIVER
It's over there.

    COP
What is?

CALIFORNIA GOTHIC

DRIVER
The body. I called in . . .

COP
We didn't get any call.
Who are you?

DRIVER
Eyeball News. We're
shooting an update on
the Olympia story . . .

COP
You mean the chemical fire?
That wasn't here.

DRIVER
I know! This is where
they hauled the cars,
after. So we're following
up, and we find this truck
—with a body in the back!

COP
Whose body?

DRIVER
I don't know! That's what
I'm telling you! Come on . . .

DENNIS ETCHISON

The COP eyes the driver up and down.

COP
Whoa. Let's see some I.D.

"Is that my dad's camera?"

Eddie lowered the Hi-8. "I guess so. I'm—holding it for him. For Tommy, I mean. He let me use it."

"He did, huh?"

"He said it was all right. Hi, Mike."

"Hi. So where is the little shit?"

"He's—" Eddie wanted to say *He's not here*, but then how could he explain why he had the camera? He waved his arm toward the acres of car parts. "He's in there."

"What are you guys doing?"

"Taking pictures."

"Of this crap?"

"Yeah. I mean no. We're—helping Raul. He said he'd pay us. To take pictures. For the insurance company. Or something."

It could be true. Mike seemed to buy it. He had heard stranger explanations for his kid brother's behavior.

"Does your mother know where you are?"

Eddie straightened to his full height, all five-foot-five inches, and answered in his most mature and responsible voice. "Yes, she does."

CALIFORNIA GOTHIC

"That's good, 'cause she came by our house before, looking for you."

"She did?" said Eddie without surprise.

"My brother said he was meeting you. But it's late, and Mom wants him. The little shit. I've got a date!"

"I'll go get him," Eddie said.

"Tell him to get his ass home right now!"

"Okay, Mike."

Eddie reentered the dark rows, aware of Mike's eyes on him. If Mike hadn't busted us, he thought, Raul would. Eddie had been in such a hurry he hadn't noticed the light in the office and the open gate. Where *was* Raul, anyway?

Surrounded by junk, he heard Mike's Explorer roar away down the street. He slowed and was about to look through the eyepiece, when the laughter came again, this time directly in front of him.

"Eddie? Is that you?"

It almost sounded like his friend's voice, but overlaid with another, higher pitch.

EXT. NIGHT - THE JUNKYARD

The COP leads the way with his flashlight. For the moment the DRIVER is left behind in the rising darkness.

> **DRIVER**
> Wait up, will you?
> (to himself)
> Where'd he go . . . ?

He makes a wrong turn in the labyrinth. Now he is lost. He feels his way along sharp edges—and lets out a curse as he *cuts his hand*. He pauses to suck the cut, then moves on . . .

DRIVER'S P.O.V. (PANAGLIDE):

The yellow glow of the COP's flashlight bobs ahead like a firefly.

Now, at the end of a huge old moving van with dented sides, we see the COP's flashlight aimed at the back of a much smaller late-model pickup truck.

The DRIVER comes up behind him.

> **DRIVER**
> The body's in there.

> **COP**
> It is, huh?

CALIFORNIA GOTHIC

ANGLE into the bed of the truck: a gas can, a Coleman chest, an empty pizza box, a backpack . . . and a sleeping bag.

> **DRIVER**
> Open it.

Skeptical, the COP reaches for the sleeping bag . . .

SOUND: *laughter*

PANNING UP—to see the GIRL as she walks forward out of the shadows beyond the truck. Her movements catlike. Her laughter hollow.

The COP shines his flashlight at the GIRL—and sees that she is *naked*.

> **COP**
> I don't suppose you have
> any I.D., either.

The DRIVER backs off.

The COP turns to him.

> COP
> Hold it. I didn't say
> you could go.

His flashlight beam follows the DRIVER, sweeping the ground . . . to show:

The CAMERAMAN's HEADLESS TORSO lying in a pool of clotted blood.

> COP
> Well, fuck me . . . !

As behind him, the GIRL climbs over the pickup truck in a single effortless movement. But she's not after the COP. Instead she goes for the DRIVER—following the trail of blood from his cut hand.

She locks his arm in a chicken-wing and clamps her mouth over his wound. Her cheeks suck in as she swallows blood.

> COP
> Freeze!

He is holding a .38 Police Special in shaky hands.

CALIFORNIA GOTHIC

She lets go of the DRIVER and drops him headfirst into the dirt. Then she faces the COP, blood greasing her chin.

When he cocks the hammer, she only laughs.

    COP
 I said—

In an instant she is on him. Driving him back into the pickup. His head strikes cold steel. His skull cracks and steaming blood runs out . . .

As the top of the sleeping bag flops open, revealing a *decomposing body* inside!

"You found us," she said.

Us? thought Eddie. He lowered the camera and opened both eyes so he could see more clearly. Without benefit of the viewfinder, however, he saw only shadows and the suggestion of form. Then there was the rectangular bed of the pickup, as dark and long as an open grave, and the golden-white circle of her face rising over it.

"Is this your truck?" he said, because he had to say something.

"It was somebody's," she said as she climbed

out on the other side. "Now it's junk, like all the rest. Nobody will ever know."

"Oh. I thought maybe you lived here, or something."

"I have a real house. A nice one. I'm moving in soon."

"When?"

"Come here. I want to show you something."

The film images were still in his mind. They jerked and blazed, streaking across the frame of his vision. He held the camera protectively at his side, where it fit in his hand like a fragile skull.

He came to the truck, felt the raised side against his chest, just below his throat. He looked over the edge, expecting to see Tommy there, laid out corpselike and ready to spring up from his hiding place with a laugh. He made out only the gas can and the ice chest and the plaid sleeping bag and the shape of what must have been a backpack. It was roughly the size of a bowling bag, the zippered sides round and bulging. What had she stuffed inside?

"Show me what?" he said.

When he looked up she was standing on the wheel-well, her body silhouetted against the sky. For a few frames her head and wild hair loomed above him, the sky behind her brightening as the moon rose, the winch and hook at the

CALIFORNIA GOTHIC

top of Raul's crane swinging over and back, over and back in the wind.

"Me," she said.

She reached across the flatbed. He drew back, afraid he would fall down into darkness.

"I can see you from here."

"What do you see?" she said, climbing into the truck.

The warm breeze blew her dress against her body so that it clung tight as a wetsuit. Every curve and muscle became visible under the thin material; she might as well have been wearing nothing. Now there were two moons in the night sky, one an oversized disk made even more enormous by the heavy air on the horizon and pale as a death's-head, the other the circle of her face with its corona of hair whipping in the wind. Then one dropped out of the sky and hovered over him as she squatted in the truck, close enough to touch.

"Who are you?" he said.

"Don't you know?"

"I don't even know your name."

"Later. If I told you now, you wouldn't believe me."

The wind grew stronger, rattling loose metal, lifting rotted upholstery from coil springs, singing through disintegrating tailpipes, running along the saw-toothed rows, laughing at him as it went away.

"Where's Tommy?"

"Does it matter?"

Yes, he thought. "I'm supposed to—give him a message."

"Forget him. He's not family."

"He's my friend."

"I'm your friend now."

"But I don't know you."

"Are you sure?"

She touched his shoulder, then slipped her hand under his armpit to coax his elbow up onto the side panel of the truck. She leaned closer, took his hand and touched it to her cheek. Her skin was cool, not like the warm wind that had brought her here. Then she turned his hand back so that her fingertips and his touched his face. He let her do that, and to draw his hand back again to her forehead and cheekbones and the whorl of her ear and her jawline and the point of her chin.

"Do you feel it?" she asked.

She placed their hands back on his face, to the shape of his head and the line of his jaw, the wispy hairs above his mouth, his lips. Then she took his index finger and touched it to the inner surface of her own lower lip, where the membrane was so slick and tender he was afraid he might hurt her.

"We're the same," she said.

So far she was right; the shape and texture

CALIFORNIA GOTHIC

was familiar enough that his skin seemed to fit against hers, cut from the same mold. For the first time in his memory nothing was required of him. It was as if he had become a part of some natural process, and that seemed enough.

"The *same*," she said.

Without knowing how, he was in the truck. The metal edge was no longer between them but the sleeping bag was hard under his foot and the backpack heavy against his leg.

"It's time," she said.

"For what?"

"Time to go."

And at that, in an instant, the bridge between them was burned. He blinked as if waking. The close-ups of her features, focused down to the pores of her skin and the flecks of color in the irises of her eyes, were lost and he was left with only his imagination, pictures that could be seen but not lived. She was just a girl again. He did not know her.

"So go," he said.

"Time for *us* to go."

"That's okay," he said. "I got stuff to do." As he found his way out of the truck, his foot bumped the backpack again. "What kind of shit do you *have* in there?" he said, to let her know that he did not care.

"Here." She opened the backpack and ex-

DENNIS ETCHISON

tracted a piece of cloth. She held it up. It was a T-shirt. "This used to be his."

"Who?" he asked.

"You can have it now."

She was crazy. *He* was crazy. He tried to get out of the truck but tripped on the sleeping bag. Was there really something inside? That part was only a movie, he told himself.

"What did you do with Tommy?" he blurted.

"Nothing."

"Then who—? I mean *what*—?"

He unzipped the bag.

"Don't you get it?" he heard her say, as he opened the flap. "It doesn't matter . . ."

Eddie saw the face of a sleeping man. At least it wasn't Tommy. *Sorry*, he started to say, but then his eyes were held by the eyes in the bag.

It was Raul. He was not awake. But he was definitely not asleep.

"The only thing that matters," she said, folding the flap closed, "is family."

He was backing away from the truck. The close-up of Raul stayed with him, growing more vivid so that colors began to show, red and brown around the edges of the long gash in the throat. Was he imagining that part? *A movie*, he told himself, *only a movie* . . .

"You didn't see anything," she said, and he almost believed her.

He staggered away until the gas tank on the

CALIFORNIA GOTHIC

side of the Peterbilt slammed into his back. He did not make a sound. She might hear even if she could no longer see him across the darkness. She might climb down after him, leap down naked against the moon, still hungry.

"None of this matters," she said. "In a few more minutes it'll be history . . ."

What's she going to do? he thought. Burn it? The wrecking yard would go up in a firestorm, with all the oil and gas . . . Not her, though. She's both of them now, twice as strong, and twice as dead. Nothing can kill her. She's here for revenge on the system that made her what she is. *She walks by night* . . .

And whether he saw or only thought he saw her strike a match then and toss it he did not know, but new images appeared on the screen of his mind, licking and twisting with tongues of fire that rose into the sky, and then the girl did leap down with superhuman strength as the clothing on her body began to burn and she kept coming and would not be stopped, her silhouette dancing translucent against the flames so that he could see the death inside her as the camera became hot in his hands.

Chapter Ten

"Do you have a gun?" asked Markham.

"Sure," said Len. "Right here under the seat. I never go out without my six-shooter." The VW bounced around the corner onto Stewart Way, valves hammering. "You think I need one?"

"I don't know. But maybe you should stop by the store and get the .38."

"Yeah, and maybe it's raining shit outside, 'cause horses have wings."

"You were there," said Markham. "You saw."

"Yeah, but I don't fucking believe it. Katie. Katie!" Len popped the transmission into neutral and coasted toward the end of the cul-de-sac. "Fucking gangs! I should have gone with her . . . I'm moving to Oregon. I'll join the Box People. Wherever the hell they are now."

"Gangs?" said Markham. "You think it was a gang?"

Len flipped the rearview mirror to the night position, so the headlights of the Toyota would not blind him. "Who do *you* think? The fuckin' CSR, back from the fuckin' grave?"

"I saw the writing on the wall, Len."

"So did I. So the fuck did I." Len hit furiously on a roach from the ashtray, his face reddening in the glow. "They got it out of a book. They don't even know what it means . . . It's like swastikas. Pentagrams. None of that shit means anything anymore. It's supposed to be cool, like the Happy Face on your lunchbox in school. That's all."

"You sure about that?"

Len cut the ignition and cranked up the hand brake as the engine chugged on for a few more revolutions, then finished the roach and ate the paper. "What the hell else does it mean? That the CSR is still out there? They're all dead. You said so yourself."

"I hope so." In the driveway, the doors of Evie's car were already swinging open. "But I think you should get the .38 anyway, after you take Jean home."

"I don't need it, Dan. And neither do you. It's not *about* you. You're not the center of the universe, remember?"

No, he thought, I'm not, but maybe somebody thinks I am. She came here. Then to the store. Katie told her about the appraisal, so she went there, too, looking for me. Maybe she thought Katie was my mistress and wanted to get rid of the competition. It fits. It could have been that way.

If so, who's next?

"Take Evie with you," he said. "I don't want her here. In case anything else happens."

"Like what?"

"I know the way her mind works."

"Whose mind are you talking about? You don't really believe that letter, do you?"

Markham looked away. In the driveway, Jean was scampering on her short legs to keep up with Evie, who was already working the front door.

"Jesus, you *do*!"

The windows along the side of the house flashed yellow as Evie ran from room to room, hitting the lights.

"All right," said Len, "what *about* the CSR? What were they? A bunch of pissant revolutionaries. They wrote a manifesto, but nobody gave a shit, because it was the middle of the seventies and they were ten years too late. And then what? They make some bombs, and the FBI comes in and burns their asses to the ground. And that's it. Just like US, MOVE, the Symbionese Fucking Jack-off Army. How many members did they have? Five? Ten? They got them all."

"It wasn't like that. Not exactly."

"Oh, then how was it? How do you know? I thought you said she joined them *after* you broke up."

"She did."

"But you knew them?"

"No, but we followed it. She liked what they had to say. They issued a statement on KPFK—the whole CSR thing was propaganda. They weren't even a Satanist church, except at the beginning, when the police invented them. They were provocateurs, paid to flush out any crazies still left over from the old days. But they turned it around and reinvented themselves as the Homefires Collective. They decided to play it out for real. That was why they had to be destroyed."

"So why didn't you sign up?"

"They believed in violence. That's where Jude and I parted company."

"And they *were* destroyed. *Weren't* they."

"Jude was the last. She never gave up."

"You're sure?"

"I'm sure."

"Say it."

"They're dead. She's dead. All right?"

"Then what happened today was some punk. Somebody who oughta be strung up by the balls."

"The guard said it was a she."

CALIFORNIA GOTHIC

"Then some gang girl or something. Who the fuck knows? It has nothing to do with you. Not a goddamned thing. Right?"

"Back off, Len."

"Right?"

"Right," he said finally.

It was easier than trying to argue from an irrational position.

Inside, Jean was at the living room phone.

"What do you want on your pizza?" she said, her mouth working overtime as usual, her eyes as untroubled by abstract considerations as the plastic beads in a doll's head, faded from the sun, with no real color or character remaining. They were eyes that had been opened to so much light for so long, so many years ago, that they could no longer see what was here, and no longer cared to see. But Markham understood what there was about Jean that had attracted Len once as he passed through his own private rituals of purification, and what appealed to Evie now: a grounding in the simplicity of the moment. The trouble was that there was no foolproof way to tell the difference between Zen emptiness and just plain empty.

"Tell them to deliver it to your place," he said.

"Why?"

He ignored her and went through to the dining room, seeing his own lot for what it was at last, as if the scales had been lifted from his eyes. He had brought Evie to a long, boatlike prefab kit that some other hopeful soul had hammered together in the forties. It had never been a dream house, not even then. And now it was falling apart despite his best efforts to fend off the inevitable, to cover the thin, narrow walls between the windows with framed broadsides and lithographs and cases of books saved like fine wines, as if these things would carry them through this life to the next, as if the knowledge they stockpiled here would continue to expand forever through time and space independently of the physical plane. He had lived too long in his head, in the abstract world, but that would no longer protect them. Perhaps Jean was more right than wrong, after all; perhaps Evie quite correctly valued her friendship as an anchor in the midst of so much impermanence.

He saw Evie ahead of him, avoiding the stacks that were in the way. She was searching for something more tangible and precious than anything here.

"Eddie . . . ?" she said.

He shouldered past the art and psychology texts and caught up with her.

"He's not in the house," she announced.

"Did you look in his room?"

But Eddie's bedroom door was open. There were no promising shapes beneath the milky plastic sheeting. At any other time she might have said something about the uncompleted paint job, but not now. She closed the door and ran for the kitchen.

The note she had left was on the table, untouched.

He found another note on the refrigerator and waved it like a winning lottery ticket.

"He's with Tommy. He'll be back later."

She read it over. That was all it said. She glanced at the oven clock as the next digital number rolled up into place: 9:51.

"It *is* later," she said.

Her eyes flicked again and again between the note, the clock and his face, retracing the simple triangulation until her position became clear.

"Evie . . ."

"I'll go get him," she said.

"Call," he said. He uncradled the phone from the wall. "Here. What's the number?"

She snatched it from him, looked at the list of numbers on the wall and cupped the receiver to the side of her head. Her lips curled in disgust.

"Hang up, Jeannie!" she said.

Across the kitchen the digital clock rolled up to 9:52. She tapped the buttons with lightning speed. He heard the insectoid music of electronic pulse tones from the imperfect seal between the handset and her ear. At 9:53 she looked up again.

"There's no answer."

"They probably went out."

"I'm going over," she said.

He did not argue with her. It simplified the equation. "Then I'll wait here, in case he comes home."

"Good," she said from the hall. She turned back. "Where's the cat?"

"I don't know."

"I haven't seen him since this morning! He always comes for dinner. But nobody was here . . ."

"Take it easy," he said. "He'll be back. I promise. He's a survivor."

"How can you promise a thing like that?" Her lips went on moving without sound for a moment and her eyes brimmed over. "He'll turn wild if we don't get him inside!"

"I'll find him."

"You'd better, that's all I can say!"

She set her jaw, turned away from him and went on to the front door.

He followed her into the living room.

"I hope they got the order . . ." Jean was saying.

He saw everything with unassailable clarity. The plywood walls you could poke a hole through with a good strong thumb. The picture

CALIFORNIA GOTHIC

frames held in place by nails that had begun bending as soon as they were tacked up. The bookcases were paper-thin veneer glued to sagging fiberboard, the furniture was kindling covered with cheap fabric as dry as the cloth used to wrap mummies. The books? They were vessels of knowledge, but only a means of transmission and not the knowledge itself, no more valuable in and of themselves than a radio signal or the sound of words spoken into the air, of symbols even weaker than flesh and unable to shield at a time like this. Why hadn't he seen it sooner?

". . . Because if they don't deliver in thirty minutes," Jean finished, "it's free!"

"Then you better get going," Markham told her.

"What about you guys?" said Jean. "We can go in two cars. Where's your kid?"

"I have to wait for him," he said.

"Then I'll ride with Eve."

"No," said Evie, and went out the front door.

"Then how . . . ?"

"Go on home," said Markham. "Please."

"Can't we at least have a drink?"

"I'm sorry," said Markham, "but I don't drink anymore. There's nothing in the house."

Lennie caught the drift. Time for the gag ball, his eyes said. "Come on, Jeannie. Start the car. I'll be right out."

"I don't understand," she said.

That's all right, thought Markham. Neither do I.

Lennie hustled her out the door and started her down the steps behind Evie, who was already at the Toyota.

"Where *is* Eddie?" he said to Markham.

"Evie's going to pick him up. I should stay, in case he gets here first."

"You need me? Jeannie can drive herself."

He considered Lennie's question, and knew that in the end his friend would do whatever he asked. Len's mind was a hemp mind, sensitized and extravagantly compassionate and dazzled by the infinity of possibilities, and if he held one to the exclusion of others it was only to make things run more smoothly or to ease another's uncertainties. It was as if the filtering mechanism that enabled him to focus on one path had dissolved long ago, so that nothing remained but wry amusement at the ultimate absurdity of it all. That was why he stayed with his pale acid queen of a wife, why he accepted the position of passive partner in the store instead of breaking away and opening another business or writing the books that were in his head, why he was content to remain a messenger boy rather than originating any messages of his own. He could do whatever he wanted but he was happy to remain lost in the funhouse. Markham loved him

CALIFORNIA GOTHIC

for what he was, a part of his past and of himself, but it was the part that could not help now.

"It's all right," he said. "Go on home."

"The cops will get her. Turn on the TV. They probably did already. Some sick gang broad."

"Yeah." Markham was surprised by Lennie's intensity, as he had been outside in the car. Where was the quip, the ironic comment that would put it all back into perspective? He could use that much from his friend at the moment. In fact he had been waiting for it.

"They'll get her ass," said Len fiercely, with red eyes. "That sick piece of . . ." He was shaking, shaking and weeping.

He did love Katie, thought Markham. Jeannie's instincts were right. He was in love with the possibility, the idea of her, twenty-two years old and golden, with a perfect life spread out before her for the tasting. She thought she had forever to choose, and so did Len. But not anymore. He's learning. And, thinking that, Markham was struck through with pity, for Katie and Lennie and Jean and Evie and himself, for all of them, and for his own son out there somewhere, trying bravely to make some sense of this world and wondering if he would be strong enough. He swallowed with great difficulty.

If they don't get her, he thought, I will.

He started to say it, but Len was already gone. As the cars drove away he walked back through the empty house, turning off every light as he went.

Come and get me.

Then he thought, Who? Who am I waiting for? A lady in a long dress, clawing her way out of the crypt like Madeline Usher, or like the one in *Isle of the Dead,* or what was her name? Barbara Steele in one of those romantic Italian horror movies, with impossibly stark eyes and moon-white forehead and praying-mantis smile above a filmy white gown?

Sure, he thought.

I'm living in a horror movie, all right. Only the horror doesn't have anything to do with necrophilia or black masses or crosses hung upside down, or with vampires who can't swim or zombies who work in sugar cane fields and can't stop shambling off cliffs when some guy with a jawbreaker accent says so. No, this is real life. It was running out all around him, the footprints of assassins and neo-fascists and government officials with secret closets full of tutus, private armies training in ships named after the wives of oilmen, of drunken Presidents in bed with the mob and cartels that slice up the world and stick FOR SALE signs on the pieces; while the real kings of the earth lie moldering in their graves, their brains stolen away in the night and their bullet wounds altered to match storybook plots that would be laughed out of any pre-

CALIFORNIA GOTHIC

school classroom. And all this while the billions sweat and grow old like the living dead, their lifeblood sucked dry by the takers of souls who need our labor to feed a hunger for power without end. The undead? What a cheapjack explanation for so much misery. There is more than enough to account for it all without falling back on the unnameable. It's already here. The trick is to see it and not flinch—there's no future in denial. It's as simple, and as enormous, as that.

The truth, however bleak, was almost comforting.

Why then, he wondered, am I still scared?

Eddie.

He's out there. But he's coming home. He's all right—he has to be. He knows to stay out of dark places and walk away from fights and not get into cars with strangers, to always wear clean underwear and not talk back to the LAPD. And he's smart, a real prodigy, who can outwrite me already and probably outthink me as well. I've taught him what I know, and his mother the things I didn't think of; between us he's equipped to handle it.

Isn't he?

Eddie, he thought. Come on home, for God's sake. That's right, boy, now. It's not so bad. We'll put on a movie, an old Ray Dennis Steckler or Coffin Joe, one of those camp classics we found out about in *Shock Zone*, and we'll laugh ourselves silly. Mom might even join us. She'll feel better when she sees you; she'll feel fine. And later I'll take her to bed and we'll be closer than we've been in months. Closer than that. Knowing you're okay.

When we move we'll have a better place, with a whole room for a big-screen TV and a top-of-the-line laser disc player. The real thing. Evie is right. We've outgrown this space the way a baby finally gets too big for the womb and has to be born—the way you were. It's not going to be that hard, after all; there are creative ways to finance. Hell, I'll liquidate Minor Arcana if I have to, sell it to Len, and he can take over the payments. He already knows the business. It can be done. I just haven't wanted to face it. This place wasn't paradise, after all, but only a stopover until we grew big enough to move on. It's time. I can handle it. It's not too late . . .

For tonight, though, this house would do. It was reality.

He made his way through it with ease, even in the dark. There was the oven to his right, its digital clock counting off the seconds and minutes with the regularity of a heart pumping through the long hours before dawn. The refrigerator next to it, humming away. Idly he hooked a finger around the door handle and tugged it open. Cool white light spilled out over the floor tiles, illuminating a checkerboard pattern that

CALIFORNIA GOTHIC

led to the back porch. There on the second shelf was an odd shape covered with lumpy foil, something he had rewrapped so many times he had forgotten what it was, the tuna casserole that no one really wanted to finish, and half a banana turning black in the cold, a container of yogurt with a scummy residue around the lip, a quart of milk. HAVE YOU SEEN THESE CHILDREN? read the public service announcement on the side of the carton, over photographs of three small faces with missing front teeth and frozen smiles. PLEASE HELP!

Eddie wasn't missing.

Of course not. Evie would bring him home any time now. She would behave as if nothing had happened, and he would hold her and help her sleep until tomorrow, Sunday, when there would be time to talk about what had happened. What was the first thing Evie would say when she walked in? Something about food; they hadn't eaten. There was hardly anything in the refrigerator but at least she wouldn't have to worry about the boy anymore. A pizza would do. First things first. Time to feed.

What about the kitten? Did he come home?

Better take care of that, before she asks.

He took the carton out of the refrigerator, poured some milk into a saucer and carried it to the service porch.

"Here, kitty kitty . . ."

He set the saucer down by the back door and waited for the cat. Outside, there was a stirring. He opened the screen door a few inches to let it in. Something low to the ground slipped into the house. He looked down and saw nothing.

The wind, he thought.

He put on the outside light, as a siren wailed in the distance.

The backyard certainly looked different now. But at least he knew where he was, and when.

There were fewer places for the kitten to hide near the house. The unpruned bushes and wild plants still filled the lot to the back fence, where just now the moon was rising, distorted to huge proportions by the soupy air over the city. He tilted his head back, exposing his face to its soothing rays, as another siren passed. There were only a few stars visible through the pollution, the handle of the Big Dipper and Venus or Jupiter twinkling on the horizon, and above it the moon, a pale, constricted face without features . . .

The moon?

Then what was the yellow ball turning orange beyond the fence?

He switched off the outdoor light for a better look, as a third siren passed in the night.

A fire?

Must be, he thought. It lit up the sky in the direction of Bradfield and the other side of town, beyond the tracks, where the sirens were headed. He hoped it was nothing serious. He seemed to feel the heat even from this far away. The Santa Ana had grown stronger now that the sun was down. That would mean sleeping with the windows up and praying for a breeze through the screens . . .

Bradfield, he thought.

The Oshidari house.

That was where Eddie had gone.

As he picked the phone from the kitchen wall, something fell with a loud thump in another part of the house.

"Evie?"

He hadn't heard her drive up.

He started into the hall.

And heard a quick, furtive scrabbling, like a small bird, on the other side of the door to his left.

The door to Eddie's room.

"Hey, Ed? You home . . . ?"

If it was Eddie, he would answer. How had he come in? He always used the back door. The window? Was he sneaking in because of the hour? That was all right. Markham was glad he was home. He closed his hand on the doorknob, then hesitated.

I should knock first, he thought. I always hated it when my dad came barging into my room.

DENNIS ETCHISON

"Is anybody there?"

The door did not want to open. He leaned on it, pushing against an invisible presence. Then something slipped around the door like a snake —the wind again. Eddie's window had to be up; that was it. The current of air subsided and the door opened the rest of the way in a rush, banging against the wall.

Before him, the plastic sheeting waved out in the breeze, then sucked back down over the room. There was the desk; was someone sitting in the chair? No, just a shadow.

Markham felt along the wall for the light switch, but it was hidden by the folds of the tarp.

A body seemed to be lying in state on the bed.

He approached, suddenly wary. A burglar? Near his knuckles, the closet door was ajar. He ignored it and squinted at the bed.

It was unmade, as always. Through the opaque plastic the lumps of twisted bedclothes appeared heavier, thicker. He put his hands out and was about to tear a hole in the plastic to be sure, when someone spoke to him from the other side.

Chapter Eleven

At first Evie did not notice how alone she was. There were no other cars in any direction; it was as if the streets between Stewart and Bradfield had been cleared so that she could get to the Oshidari house in record time. Even the elementary schoolyard was deserted, without the usual cast of hardnosed kids shooting baskets inside the fence at all hours. The blacktop was empty under the security lights, and not a single tagger walked the flat roof or lurked in the shadows with a can of spray paint, ready to add his magic emblem to the stucco facade.

The deserted intersection below the tracks invited her to run the stop sign. She coasted up and over the first hump with only a cursory glance at the rails ahead. There was no sign of a locomotive beam to the right or left of her car but only darkness. She rolled through the red light and started to make a turn, when a horn almost blasted her off the road.

She hit the brake and pushed away from the steering wheel, elbows locking, and gaped at the rearview mirror. Behind her, a black corridor extended all the way back to the playground, where the security lights now defined the edges of the buildings, transforming them into the sharp, jagged pattern at the end of a kaleidoscope. Then she focused past the mirror as a fire engine tore across the intersection, inches from her front bumper.

Only then did the siren go on.

Evie watched the red-and-silver streak pass. Her hands gripped the wheel so tightly that she expected it to fracture in her hands. She stopped squeezing and her skin came unstuck, deformed into white ridges where the wheel had been. Her fingers felt numb, with black plastic curled up under the nails.

Now breathe, she told herself.

The fire engine braked a few blocks down and turned left to cross the tracks, away from the residential streets. At least it was not on its way to the Oshidari house. She saw the long vehicle slow to a stop as it negotiated the turn, leaving the rear section jackknifed so that it blocked the full width of the street. How many precious seconds or minutes would it take for her to get around it? Better not take the risk. She could

CALIFORNIA GOTHIC

cross the tracks here, turn onto the boulevard and then cut back farther down, at the next light. She looked both ways, proceeded cautiously over the rails, and made a right.

There was no traffic here, either. The chain restaurants were all brightly lighted, many of them with cars still in the lots, but no one appeared to be driving in or out. All four lanes of the boulevard were clear as far as she could see, which was not more than a few blocks because of the fog ahead.

Fog? How could that be? The wind had blown the sky clear, and it was the wrong time of the year for fog, anyway. Yet the air over the signs was opaque, and now precipitation began to fall onto her windshield. When she activated the wipers the glass did not come clean. The blades only pushed the particles down into fuzzy lines. Then she saw more particles settling over the hood, and realized they were ashes.

The sky grew yellow.

Now she noticed police cars at every intersection, blocking traffic. The streets beyond, toward the mall, were aglow with bumper-to-bumper headlights, dim candles in a dust storm. There were more fire trucks slewed up to the chain-link fence that ran in front of the old wrecking yard, and above them the yellow sky was turning orange.

The Pick-A-Part was on fire!

DENNIS ETCHISON

She drove around the trucks as men in protective clothing unfolded a canvas hose like a starved boa constrictor and connected it to a hydrant. At the end of the long block, at the first corner, she veered over to find a way to cross the tracks, but a policeman stepped out into the street and waved his arms, shaking his head. She waved back and started past him, and saw that the next intersection was blocked as well. She stopped and lowered her window.

"Off the street!" he shouted before she could say a word.

"I was just trying to—"

"Now!"

She leaned her head out and forced her lips into a smile. "I live here. On—" What was the name of the Oshidaris' street? "On Bradfield," she lied. "I have to get home. I—"

He did not want to hear any of it.

"Move it, ma'am, or I'll have to cite you."

"You don't understand. I saw the fire, and I drove over. Now I'm trying to get back home. If you'll tell me where to turn around . . ."

"No turns."

Did he really have his hand on his holster? She retained her smile. "If you won't let me turn, how can I get back?"

"You can't. Clear the area!"

She pointed past him, in the direction of the mall. "Is Wibberly open?" But even as she spoke

CALIFORNIA GOTHIC

she saw more black-and-whites moving into place ahead. "What street can I take?"

He placed one hand on her left front fender as though to stop her with brute force. His other hand came to rest on the grip of his revolver. "Wait at the pizza parlor," he ordered. "We'll let you know when it's clear."

There was no way to reason with him. He was still young and playing his part for all it was worth. His eye sockets were deep tunnels with no chance of light at the end. If she ran the roadblocks, he might crouch instinctively and open fire with armor-piercing bullets. It was absurd, but she had ventured into occupied territory without the proper credentials. She could not even show him her I.D. to prove where she lived; she had said Bradfield, but her driver's license said Stewart Way. There was no hope.

"Thank you, Officer," she said, and backed up just enough to aim her front wheels at Reggae Rat's, a hundred yards farther along the boulevard.

I'll park, she thought, and call Mrs. Oshidari again. There'll be a pay phone inside. Or I'll slip out and make it across on foot. They wouldn't shoot an unarmed woman, would they? A mother?

First I should call home and see if Eddie's there.

The lot was packed with cars waiting for the

all clear, their tops rippling with an amber glaze. She nosed into a handicapped space, the only one left, got out and saw her hands and arms change color, an unnaturally pale, jaundiced yellow. Across the street and down the block, the sky above the old wrecking yard glowed as if a new sun were about to rise out of the ground. She heard shouts from inside the fence and more sirens closing in. Then the sky blackened with plumes of smoke and more ashes blew this way, a cloud of fireflies descending over the great rat-god's winglike ears. She snatched her purse off the seat and ran inside.

The restaurant was full, a few families and working men but mostly teenagers, sprawled in the booths and joking manically as they swallowed strings of pizza cheese and sucked on Cokes. PLEASE WAIT TO BE SEATED, said a sign by the hostess station, but no one was there. The employees were huddled by the counter in their ridiculous taupe vests, while a solitary child, a little girl, manipulated the remote-controlled claw on a machine in the Mouse Gallery, determined to snag a plush doll from a rat's nest of artificial cheese wedges.

"Where's your telephone?" Evie said loudly.

The employees ignored her, the teenagers cracked jokes and the little girl slugged another Mouse Token into her machine. Evie spotted a hallway and a plaque with the toothy, winking

CALIFORNIA GOTHIC

face of Reggae Rat himself pointing the way to the Mouser and Mousette restrooms. That, she deduced, was where the phone would be. She started for the hall.

A boy sat in the last booth, reading a copy of *Shock Zone Magazine*.

She knocked it out of his hands in order to see his face.

"Oh, Tommy," she said, disappointed.

He avoided meeting her eyes, looking nervously past her. "Hello, Mrs. Markham. Where's Eddie?"

"I thought he was with you."

"He was."

"*Was?*"

"He's supposed to meet me. But he didn't make it."

She didn't believe that for a second. "What's your number?" she demanded, digging in her purse.

"You mean my phone number? Why?"

"Because I'm calling your mother."

"I tried that," he said. "She must be asleep already."

The way he slumped down in the booth then, fingering the magazine pages without looking at them, she knew that part was probably true. His face was dirty and his clothes were disheveled, torn at the shirt cuffs, with one of the buttons missing. There was even a dark stain like grease or soot on his shoulder.

"If he's not at your place," she said, "and he's not here, where is he?"

"Are you mad at him?"

"No," she said, and meant it. "I just want to know where he is."

"Me, too."

"What are you doing here?"

"They won't let anybody go anywhere," he said. "I tried, but they busted my ass. My butt, I mean."

"Don't move," she said. "I want to talk to you."

She went into the hall. There was a line at the wall phone. It would take too long. She returned to the booth, more frustrated than ever.

She shouldn't lay it all on the boy. He looked like he had been through enough already.

"Where did you go tonight?" she asked. "You and my son. To another movie?"

"Yeah. No. We just went—out. You know."

"What happened?"

He made an exaggerated shrug, like a much younger boy caught playing hooky. That endeared him to her. She did not want to play teacher.

"We—sort of had to hide for a while. There were these guys. From high school."

She tensed. "What did they do to you?"

"Nothing. I mean, we got away."

CALIFORNIA GOTHIC

If he was lying again, covering up for her benefit, the truth must be worse. "Where did you hide?"

Tommy's studied, expressionless manner weakened under her gaze, as if he knew that it was all too simplistic to be believable, even to an adult. He faltered, measuring his words, as though seeking to add only the most neutral details.

"We were going to my house. We saw these guys we know. They said, 'Our car won't start,' so we go, 'We'll help you.' I—I pushed it, but it still wouldn't start. So they got pissed off. Mad, I mean. She chased us, but we got away."

The end, she thought. Tell me another one. What a load of rubbish. Who does he think he's talking to? Is his mother as dotty as she seems?

"Oh? And what happened to Eddie?"

"Eddie?" That threw him. He had left out an important plot point in his little melodrama.

"You don't know."

"No," said Tommy with the haughty innocence of a straight-A student discovered drilling a peephole into the girls' gym. "He went home. That's what I thought."

The thin overlay of Tommy's whitewash was beginning to wear through. He was slipping, the weakest pieces of the cover-up exposed in the unforgiving light of the swag lamp over his head.

"I thought he was meeting you," she said.

"Yeah. I mean, he was going to. Originally."

The Oshidari boy looked over his shoulder, at the breaking point and ready to bolt. In the next booth a scrawny seventeen-year-old with a rude T-shirt draped his arm around the neck of a deliberately pale girl with dyed black hair.

Evie's eyes refused to release Tommy from his seat. "You said 'she.'"

"When?"

The scrawny boy lit a cigarette with one hand and lowered his other hand over the pale girl's breast with the same purposeful calculation as the child working the mechanical claw at the rat's nest machine by the door. "*She* chased you. Who's *she*?"

"I don't know, Mrs. Markham."

"I think you do." Evie was tensing up again, and it was not only the sirens or the smoke outside or the flames in the sky. She could not sustain this tiresome interrogation, no more than she could tolerate the blatantly lascivious passivity of the girl in the next booth. "Let's cut through this, all right? What girl?"

"Well, I don't know her name . . ."

I don't either, thought Evie. I never asked. "What did she look like?"

"Just a girl."

"Did she have long hair?"

"Short."

CALIFORNIA GOTHIC

So he had decided to tell the truth. "And she wore a kind of long dress," said Evie. "They used to call them shifts. Thin material, with a simple, nonrepresentational pattern, and her eyes were—" How to say it? "Dead."

Tommy's eyes dilated, made smaller by his glasses but wide open, alert and unabashedly intelligent. Precocious. Like Eddie.

"She was nice," he told Evie. "Then the fire started. So I hauled ass out of there. Eddie, too, I guess. I didn't see which way he went."

"Eddie thought she was nice?" she said.

"It wasn't what you think." But he blushed anyway, which told her more than she wanted to hear. "It was just a game."

"Where?" She held his wrist to the table in case he was thinking of leaving. "Oh, shit," she said, "you mean the Pick-A-Part, don't you? My God!"

Tommy didn't answer. But that was why he was waiting, waiting and watching the door. He was no more sure than she was that her son was safe.

An explosion rocked the street outside. The plate glass windows bowed inward under the shock waves, about to break. Across the street a pillar of fire shot into the sky, encircled by a smoke ring that rose up and up.

"Radical," said the girl in the next booth.

Evie was already through the door. The fire

now raged out of control, lighting the skeletal chain-link fence as black smoke roiled across the sky. A hot wind struck her, dessicating her skin. She rubbed her arms to protect them from the heat, and felt crisp, burnt hairs breaking off and rolling like iron filings under her palms. Tommy was right there with her. More fire trucks were on their way from other parts of the city, sirens rising and falling, and somewhere dogs howled like wild coyotes. Somewhere doors slammed and people cried out, and cars smashed into one another as traffic everywhere screeched to a stop, and then the heavy organic smell of burning rubber and bubbling oil blew down, carrying white-hot particles that settled over the helmets of the men in canvas coats and the policemen and their cars, over the black statue of Reggae Rat, filling his arms with a benediction of ashes, coating the street like the heavy flakes from a crematorium, and the horizon lit up as if the city, the county and the world were about to go up in smoke. At the far curb hoses inflated and spat with a great writhing and hissing and men ran into the grounds of the wrecking yard, but no one came out.

Now, under the firelit sky, with this section of the boulevard cordoned off at both ends and the giant upright rat on his elevated guard tower, Evie thought of a prison or concentration camp under powerful searchlights that rendered es-

CALIFORNIA GOTHIC

cape out of the question. She sized up her chances, which were all but nil.

The firemen and police were clotted at the open gate of the inferno; for the moment no one was watching the road. She decided to try it.

"Mrs. Markham, don't!"

That was Tommy. He should wait, she thought. He'll be safe here.

She got to the opposite curb and the end of the fence. It cut back to the tracks at a right angle to the boulevard, marking the western perimeter of the wrecking yard. Inside, sleeping engines awoke in the firestorm, a long truck breathed flames from its dragon mouth, tires reduced to pools of magma and the fumes of vaporized gasoline billowed out of the yard in a cellophane mirage. She called her son's name but her voice was lost to the roar. When she touched the fence the links seared a diamond pattern into her hands and she smelled scorched flesh.

What about the other end of the lot? Had the fire spread that far? Or was Eddie hunkered there in an air pocket, waiting for a chance to climb out?

She could not get around the back. Sparks blew hot tracers across the tracks; patches of wild grass and Scotch broom were already igniting in front of the houses below. She retreated to the boulevard.

The knot of police and firefighters drew tight at the gate. Inside, a hook-and-ladder truck served as a base of operations. Every face was turned to the conflagration, red as sun worshippers, but if she tried to get past them she would surely be spotted and detained.

She heard shouts behind her, a commotion at the western roadblock, and now a renegade Ford Explorer broke through the barrier. Police dove aside as the vehicle sheared off the front end of a squad car and charged ahead.

At the front of the pizza parlor, Tommy stepped off the curb.

The van swerved around him.

"Here!" yelled Tommy.

The driver hit the brakes hard and the van nosed down, scraping the pavement.

Tommy jumped up onto the passenger side.

Evie waved her arms. "Wait!"

The driver wore a high school letterman's jacket. He straight-armed the wheel and floored the accelerator, and the vehicle lurched forward.

Boots pounded asphalt and she thought she saw the glint of a gun barrel as officers ran to catch up.

Ahead, a crowd of uniforms clogged the street in front of the wrecking yard. Tommy's brother sounded the horn.

CALIFORNIA GOTHIC

"Don't hit 'em, Mike . . . !" yelled Tommy.

"Move, you dumb asses!"

The officers scattered as the van bore down on them. All but one young cop, the one who had stopped Evie a few minutes ago. He unsnapped his holster and raised his revolver with both hands.

At the last instant the driver yanked the wheel to one side, just enough to miss the cop, and picked up speed.

The roadblock at Remar was not yet completely closed. Most of the officers fell back to their positions at the blockades. But the young cop dropped down to a shooter's stance and braced his wrist on his knee. She saw the flash of the report, and then one of the rear tires blew out. The van fishtailed, teetering on two wheels. It might have stayed up if both rear tires were still there but a bare rim touched the blacktop and gouged out a spray of sparks. The van tipped over and caromed to a stop.

Had Tommy jumped free in time?

Evie ran to help.

"Tommy . . . !"

He picked himself up and crawled away from the van. "Where's Mike?"

She leaned against the toppled van, shaken. Then she started around the steaming front end, and saw the driver.

"Here!" she said.

He lay sprawled on the pavement next to the open window. He looked like he was asleep with his face on his arms. Tommy pulled at his jacket, turning him over.

Mike groaned and sat up.

"End run . . . God damn it, you little shit! Mom wants you home *now*!"

"Don't move him," said Evie.

"Who's she?" said Mike.

"Eddie's mom."

"I'll get an ambulance . . ."

"He's okay," said Tommy. "Go on. I'll take care of him."

She heard the boots drawing near. A few more seconds and they would be here. She would be arrested. They all would be. It might take hours.

"I can't just leave," she said.

"Go on," said Tommy.

"What about you?"

"I have to stay with my brother."

He's right, she thought. Family is what matters. We have to stay together. There's no one else. Eddie. And Dan. Me. We only have each other. That's all there is.

There were no police around the van, not yet. To the north, by the railroad tracks, a footpath led down to a shallow ravine and up the other

CALIFORNIA GOTHIC

side, back to Remar and the elementary school and the streets that would lead her home.

If she did not go now, right now, she realized, there would be no possible way of finding out before morning what had happened to her son.

Chapter Twelve

All he wanted to do was go to sleep.

He got his shoulders through the window and wriggled in, clutching the camera. The pillow cushioned his fall and the sheets were almost cool, but that would not last. The air in his room would soon be as hot as the night outside. It had followed him.

Eddie buried his face in the pillows. He stayed that way till he had trouble breathing, then rolled over onto his back. Where were the glow-in-the-dark stars on his ceiling? He had pasted them there as a child, using the stepladder, with his father's help. They did not follow the constellations in any book but a pattern known only to himself, one that provided a reference point, an anchor when he turned off the lamp. Even when he went to sleep lying on his stomach or his side he knew that they were there and would not change their course during the night. Now the sky above his head seemed overcast, with no stars to tell him that he was really home. Was it because the light had been off for so long that the luminous ink needed recharging, or was the soot from outside in his room, as well?

It was his father's fault. The plastic was still up, covering everything, a canopy like mosquito netting over his bed. Dad had made so many promises and broken them; this was only one more. For now, Eddie just wanted to block it all out and sleep. They would not even know he was here when they came home. It was better that way. He closed his eyes and drifted.

A montage of images and colors appeared on his eyelids.

Blankets.

A Coleman chest.

A backpack.

A gasoline can . . .

And within a sleeping bag, the face of an old wino, as red as chopped meat. The oozing features morphed into the face of Raul, the night man—no, the owner of the Pick-A-Part—cold and dead with his eyes fixed on the stars over the junkyard; the stars faded out one by one until there were none, only the dust blowing across the sky, tinting everything yellow, and through it all another face, smooth and beautiful, shining down on him. He could not escape her. She tracked him wherever he went, growing brighter like the smoldering cars around him and the ground at his feet, following him home . . .

Now he heard her naked footsteps in the hall, on the other side of his door.

How long had he been asleep? A second? A minute?

He rolled over.

The door bulged toward him, breathing. Or did it? The plastic sheet filled with air from the window and ballooned out, then sank back.

His door was still closed and there was no one in the hall.

His parents had not come home. He would have heard them drive up.

Then why was the doorknob moving?

It turned, a small round planet rotating in the darkness. Then the wind came up again, blowing over him, filling the room and holding the door shut. But someone was trying to get through from the other side and they would not give up. The door strained on its hinges.

"What do you want from me?" he said.

The wind subsided, the door opened and a dark figure walked in.

"Is that you?" The figure had his father's voice.

"Yeah." When had Mom and Dad come home? Eddie scooted away from the end of the bed and pushed back into the pillows at the headboard. "Leave me alone."

The shadow floated closer and sat in the chair, stretching the plastic membrane between them to the breaking point, and through the taut layers the eyes of the model kits on the shelves behind his desk stood out more clearly in the glow from the window, except for the one of Michael Myers, which had no eyes in its killer's mask, only blank holes.

"Where were you?"

"With Tommy. Okay?"

"Where?" He heard the tension in his father's voice, and the unspoken accusation.

"At his house, I said."

"Nobody's home at Tommy's."

"How do you know?"

"Your mother called."

Sure, she did. Checking up on me. If she even cared.

"We went out, I said."

"No, you said you were at your friend's house."

"So we went for a walk." Leave me alone, he thought. Please.

"Did you see the fire?"

It was a trick question. He knows where I went, thought Eddie. "Yeah. So?"

"Well, what happened?"

Now he *is* accusing me. I'm a firebug. What

am I supposed to say? *We were playing with matches. We're just a couple of little kids. What do you expect?*

"I don't know, Dad. I'm in bed now. Good night."

"Talk to me."

The window was bright now, as if it were morning. He felt like he had not slept in a long time. Because his father would not let him.

"I don't want to talk."

"Well, I do, damn it!"

"Why? What do you care?"

"What did you say?"

"I said, so what? I can take care of myself."

His father rose up and punched a hole in the plastic. His face had angry stripes on it. The light outside the window was red and the breeze blew in over them both, hot and smelling of steam. A haze clouded the air. Eddie's eyes burned.

"We were very worried about you." His father was breathing hard to keep from coughing.

"Well, I'm okay. Why don't you have a drink or something?"

A fist struck Eddie on the side of the head.

Shocked, he kicked away into the corner, ready to go out the window.

"Sorry," his father said without meaning it. "I shouldn't have done that. It's not your fault— you don't know anything about it . . . Look.

Your mother's been crazy, she's so worried . . ."

Not you, thought Eddie.

His father sat on the bed.

"I don't know where to start. I can't tell what's real anymore . . ."

More sirens cut through the night. The glow outside, beyond the fence, was redder now and the air blowing in was laced with smoke and bits of ash.

"I don't know anything about the fire, okay? I saw it, and I came home. All right?"

His father eyed him suspiciously. "I didn't say you started it. I know that. What I'm asking you is, Do you know who did?"

"Some girl."

"What girl?"

He doesn't believe me. Is he going to hit me again?

"I don't know. I saw her there—"

"Where?"

"The Pick-A-Part. All I know is—"

"What did she look like?"

"She didn't look like anything."

"Smooth skin, like butter, and eyes—eyes that . . ."

The smoke had spread out, expanding, taking shape in the air from floor to ceiling, as real as if someone were standing behind his father

CALIFORNIA GOTHIC

right now, halfway between the bed and the door. And eyes. Eddie saw eyes in the smoke.

"You always liked my eyes," she said, "didn't you, Danny?"

Chapter Thirteen

"What do you want from me?"

"Is that you?" He recognized the voice. It was Eddie's voice, of course.

"Yeah."

Now he saw his son's head in wavery silhouette. God bless him, thought Markham. He wanted to cross the room and tear through the plastic dropcloth and hug him, but that would embarrass them both. At least his son was safe.

"Where were you?" he said gently. With a girl? The idea made him grin. Climbing in after hours so that no one would notice. That's not necessary. You can tell me. I'll understand. If your mother doesn't, I'll explain it to her.

"With Tommy, *okay?*"

Defensive. Well, I would be, too. I was, in fact, when I had something to keep from my parents.

"Where?" he said, to make conversation. He

wanted only to let his son know that it was all right.

"At his house, I said."

Come on, Eddie boy, out with it. I can handle the truth.

"Nobody's home at Tommy's," he said, smiling secretly. You see? You can't fool your old dad.

"How do you know?"

"Your mother called." That was reasonable enough, considering the hour. You should have thought of that. Let me help you with your story, so you'll have the answers she wants to hear.

Eddie chose to stonewall him. "We went out, I said."

Follow my logic, he thought. It's preparation for the kinds of questions you're going to get a lot more of from now on. "No, you said you were at your friend's house."

"So we went for a walk!"

The boy wouldn't break.

Time to change the subject.

"Did you see the fire?"

"Yeah. So?"

No accusation intended. Jesus, she must be something. "Well, what happened?"

"I don't *know*, Dad. I'm in bed now. Good night."

"Talk to me?" he suggested.

CALIFORNIA GOTHIC

"I don't want to talk!"

"Well, I do." He sounds just like me. Not my best side, either. Why is that always the way? "Damn it," he said to himself.

"Why? What do *you* care?"

The boy was only trying to establish his independence. That was normal. But Markham wanted to look him in the eyes, to show him his own eyes and the normal concern there. Eddie was intelligent. He would be able to see it.

"We were very worried about you . . ."

Then Eddie said something dumb, about an old problem that didn't exist anymore, and the next thing Markham knew he had ripped away the barrier between them and hit his son upside the head.

As soon as he did it he was sorry. He cupped his hand around the boy's head to cancel the gesture, but Eddie pulled away.

He doesn't like me very much right now, Markham thought. It wasn't the boy's fault. How to explain? He didn't know where to start. After today it was hard to know what was real.

Take it one step at a time.

The sirens outside, they were real.

And the girl Eddie wouldn't talk about. He imagined her, but the picture startled him. What was the picture in Eddie's mind? It wouldn't be the same. It couldn't be. Eddie's girl would be different. Not skin like butter, or eyes that—

"You always liked my eyes," said a voice he did not know, *"didn't you, Danny?"*

It was only a voice inside his head.

Then what was Eddie staring at?

Something behind him, in the hall.

"How did *she* get in?" said Eddie. He sounded genuinely alarmed. "Dad . . . ?"

Markham put a finger to his lips and motioned for Eddie to stay put, just to stay the hell where he was, until he could find out how real she was.

The hall was empty.

She's real.

She's not real.

Either way, you've got to face it. Whatever it is. It ends here.

He went to the kitchen and switched on the light.

The back door stood open a few inches, the way he had left it. The screen door, too.

So she had let herself in.

Why the back door?

Had she been here before?

Then he thought, She?

Who is *she?*

He concentrated on the details before him.

The yard outside was tipped with orange

CALIFORNIA GOTHIC

from the fire across town and a vortex of smoke blew over the horizon like the contrail of an aborted missile launch at sunset, pink and purple and cottony white.

On the ground, a small, dark shape held the screen door ajar, next to the saucer of milk he had left for the kitten.

A backpack.

Eddie's?

He had never seen it before. He picked it up by the strap and carried it into the kitchen and was about to open the top, when he heard what might have been laughter from another part of the house.

The door to his son's room was still closed.

Now the mock laughter again, from the direction of the dining room.

The books and videotapes were all in their places on the dark shelves and the lump on the table was only a bowl of fruit. Sirens warbled in the distance.

Across the living room, the front door remained locked.

Someone giggled again, closer.

He entered the main bedroom, thinking: I could turn on the light. The switch is here on the wall, under my hand.

If I do, what will I see?

He touched the switch, playing with it, caressing it like a knob of warm flesh. Up is on, down is off . . .

Then he did not have to choose, because he saw her eyes. They were yellow in the firelight that flashed through the side of the house.

Once, he thought, I saw those eyes in the campus bookstore. They were poring over titles, and they came to rest on the fringes of the Political Science section, where *Steal This Book* and *Soul on Ice* and *The Glass House Tapes* and *The Anarchist's Cookbook* could be found. She pulled down one title after another, scanning and discarding, as though looking for something that had not yet been written. He had only Rilke's *Letter to a Young Poet* in his hand, along with Maugham's *The Summing Up*, the Mentor edition, and William Carlos Williams's *Paterson* in paperback, too, because that was all he could afford, but none of these was the sort of thing that would help her. Later he saw her at the RCP rally that almost no one attended, and she came up and asked him quite bluntly if he was following her because he was a cop. That was how it started.

Five days later she came over with all her things in the car, and for the next four years they were never apart. When they weren't at the movies they would stay up late reading to each other, he from *The Essential Lenny Bruce* or Philip K. Dick or maybe one of David Thomp-

CALIFORNIA GOTHIC

son's graceful, ironic essays in *Film Comment*, she from *Fire in the Streets* or Fanon or Camus, especially *Resistance, Rebellion and Death*, her favorite. When she moved into the collective he almost went with her but finally could not, and they argued and then cried together and made promises, it would only be for a while, he would not stand in the way of her freedom and she'd be back, and then she was gone. When he went to the warehouse to visit he found her shacked up with someone on the second floor and after that he never went back. Later he thought he saw her at a demonstration outside a Vietnam War movie in Century City and then at a Pink Floyd concert, her eyes dancing from laser beam to beam under the light show, but they were different eyes by then, the bright brown veined with yellow and more stark without the long hair to hide them. And then the news stories about the CSR and the burnout, napalm and a Vietnam-style tank modified with a battering ram, and Evie came into the picture. But there had never been a clean break and the memory of Jude lingered like the phantom image of an amputated limb. That went on until Eddie was born and it was finally over . . .

Or so he had thought.

"Jude?" he said, the sound of her name barely a whisper.

The sheets rustled and long legs and a body

materialized on the bed, pale as ectoplasm in the yellow light.

"I promised you I'd come back . . ."

"*How?*"

"You didn't believe that story about the fire, did you?" She seemed to rise from the bed, or was she only sitting up? Then she giggled, younger and more girlish even than he remembered her, but now he realized what was so peculiar about the sound. It was humorless.

"But the body—"

"Just some girl. A runaway. Those were her fingerprints on the gun. It was the only thing that didn't burn."

A hostage? He hadn't even known there were any. No one had known.

He left the doorway and came closer.

"What do you want?"

"Only what's mine."

But there was no room for her here. The emptiness inside him was cauterized and healed over and other flesh had taken her place, living flesh that had made him whole again. Any attempt to displace what he had now would be an invasion by something alien, a cancer that had to be cut off.

"I have a family now."

She got to her knees on the bed, and he saw that she was naked.

"I don't," she said. "I don't have anything. I've

CALIFORNIA GOTHIC

been waiting a long time . . . You owe me, Danny."

Where have you been hiding? he thought. On a mountaintop? In a cave? Or right here in the city, under an assumed name? And now you walk into my life again. As if you could do that.

"That was years ago," he said. "Everything's different."

"That's not what you said in your letters."

"What letters?"

"The ones you wrote after you left."

"After *I* left?"

"They're all I've had," she continued. "And your picture. You've changed, Danny."

Of course I have, he thought. But you haven't. Your eyes, your face, your body . . . the same. *Exactly.*

He looked at her in the yellow light, and knew that she was not what she appeared to be. She couldn't be.

"Who are you?"

"I'm the fire in your heart. The fire that never dies!"

What if it were true? If you had come back to me before I met Evie, how would my life be different? Would we have lived on the run, always hiding, like shadow people, while everything around us changed and we did not? What kind of life would that have been? You who could kill as if it were your birthright, and burn an innocent girl beyond recognition and leave her fingers wrapped around an automatic weapon that belonged to you while you made your escape . . . to what? You would have left your mark. A robbery here, a beating there, a murder when it was necessary to survive—wouldn't that have altered the world? Would it be any better? Would it really? How do you know? And you, what would you have become? It would have changed you, that fugitive life. Do you think you could have remained so beautiful through it all? Wouldn't you have become something else, something that even you would no longer recognize in the mirror?

No, he thought, it's not possible.

"I asked you a question. Who are you?"

"Don't you remember, my love?"

"You were some girl. I thought I knew you, but I didn't."

"You're wrong. I'm more than that. More than you know."

She lay back on the bed in the half-light.

"And now I've come home, Danny, to the place where I belong . . ."

"Would you kill for that? For what you think is yours?"

"Wouldn't you?"

"No. But you did, didn't you? It was only a few hours ago. Her name was Katie. She was just a girl, too. You thought she was in the way."

CALIFORNIA GOTHIC

"It wasn't me."

"Liar," he said.

"I've been close to you all day, waiting . . ."

"Liar!" He crossed the room and grabbed her. The skin was so cool, so smooth, so much more youthful than his or Evie's. "Liar!"

She put her hands around his neck and drew him down to her.

There is a chemistry in skin. It is in the pores and in the layers underneath the pores, in the molecules that make every body different from all others, except those that spring from a common source. A river may run long and wide and branch into smaller streams, but the water smells the same and tastes as sweet no matter where the current takes it . . .

He knew Evie's flavor and the aroma of her skin and, though he loved it, it was not the same as his own.

His son's, however, ran true, through all the years of dirt and sweat and baths. It was diluted but he always knew it, just as he knew the warm tang of his own blood from a paper cut or the smell of his shirts in the closet. It was there when he had kissed Eddie in his crib and later when the boy slept between them in the big bed.

He had forgotten Jude's smell until now.

The lips opening under his tasted of smoke and copper and something else that was familiar, an echo of the original, one generation removed. The scent was one that he knew almost as well as Eddie's. And that could not be.

He knew her.

He did not know her.

Both statements could not be true.

"I wouldn't lie to you," she said as she held him. "I'm your one, your only one . . ."

He pushed her away. "My what?"

"Your lover."

He slapped her.

"Your little girl."

He slapped her again.

"Don't you know me?" she said, as though she did not feel the blows.

He backed away from her on the bed.

"What's your name?" he said. "Say it!"

"My mother called me Susan. She said you'd like it."

"She wasn't pregnant," he said, struck by the full weight of what she was saying. "I would have known."

She giggled again, mechanically. "Are you sure?"

"Where is she? Where is your mother?"

"She died. I finally burned her body. After I had learned it all, everything she knew. Especially about you. I needed to grow strong, so I'd be ready. Well, I'm ready now . . ."

His life, the construct he had built so carefully and had lived in for the last few years col-

CALIFORNIA GOTHIC

lapsed around him, shattered into pieces that would blow away on the wind. He needed time to take in this new reality, but knew that his time was all used up.

"I'll give you a few minutes," he said, "before I call the police. That's all I can do. Maybe you'll make it."

But watch out for a guy named Lennie, he thought. He won't care who you are.

"I don't have to hide anymore," she said. "We can be a real family now. And there are others . . . They've been waiting, too. We'll finish what she started . . ."

Her voice was flat, affectless, a parody of a California girl. She spoke as if reciting a recipe or reading from *TV Guide*. She wanted, she acted; in the final analysis there were no other considerations.

Like Jude.

"Get out," he said.

"What? You can't just . . ."

"Can't I?"

He thought: If you stay I'll pound your ass raw, little girl, with my hands, these hands right here, like your mother should have but never did, your crazy mother, and you'll learn to face the music for the first time in your life. Will you? We'll see.

"Listen to me, you little bitch!" he said, and dove for her across the bed.

"What are you doing?" she said, planting her feet firmly apart, refusing to flinch. "You can't hurt me! I'm your—"

He slapped her across the mouth this time, drawing blood.

She touched her mouth, looked at her fingers, then at him.

"You hurt me," she said, astonished.

He felt rage rising, his heart thumping, his neck and scalp prickling. He took her wrist and flung her across the room. But she was tall and strong and stayed on her feet. She tilted her head to one side.

"Why?"

"Out!"

"Where? I'm home!"

He thought he heard the front door open.

"Home?" said Evie, coming up behind her. "Whose home? *Get out of my bedroom!"*

Evie swung as hard as she could, landing a fist in the girl's back.

The girl stumbled, straightened her shoulders and turned. She opened one hand and when her fingers closed they were around Evie's throat.

Evie had the presence of mind to throw her weight forward instead of resisting, and that forced the girl back. They tumbled onto the bed, Evie on top, tearing hair until the fingers let go of her neck. She kept pulling, pushing, driving the skull against the headboard.

Now the girl had a knife in her hand.
"Drop it!"
Markham helped Evie wrestle the arm back.
The free hand poked at Evie's eyes. Evie let go but Markham slammed the other wrist into the headboard until the girl released the knife.

When Evie went at her again, the knife came up in the other hand. The blade, long and honed to a quicksilver edge, snicked the air, slashing Evie across the midriff.

Before the knife could slash again, Markham's mind snapped into perfect focus, calm as a reed in the eye of a storm. He saw Evie's body in relation to the girl's, the wrists and arms and the angles of their elbows, the positions of the faces, each the cobra and each the mongoose, so precisely that it might have been happening in slow motion. He interposed himself between them, sure that she would not kill him. And it was true; the blade froze in midthrust, hanging as weak as a rubber knife from her wrist, and her yellow eyes scanned him without blinking, merely noting and recording, as he shook his head *no*. For an instant he remained there, protecting them from each other, as the light of the fire outside washed over them all. He did not have to turn his head to know that Evie was climbing off the bed, because he could see every increment of the motion in the brass discs of his daughter's insane eyes.

DENNIS ETCHISON

The girl named Susan moved to her right, he moved to his left, a perfect dance. Who was leading and who following? The synchronization was so exquisite that for the first time he understood the meaning of the word *simultaneous*, a concept that was beyond the power of any word to convey. He merged with it and became it, his coordination more precise than it had ever been before.

His wife was off the bed. So was he. The girl moved toward her and he was there to block the knife. He began to feel that he could go on forever like this, maintaining the balance between them, when he lost control of his left arm.

It hung stiff and bloated at his side, pulling on the socket in his shoulder till his neck hurt between the chin and collarbone. The muscles there were threatening to tear loose. He attempted to lift the arm with his right hand to relieve the pressure but too late, the pain was sharper now, squeezing his chest. His eyes blurred and his feet lost contact with the floor and he fell forward, an unplanned body block the girl could not have anticipated. It knocked her sideways, against the windows. Then the yellow light went out and all he could hear was the sound of his own blood as loud as exploding glass in his ears.

When the light came on it was bright white and he was on the floor, shivering.

CALIFORNIA GOTHIC

"Daddy?"

Eddie's voice. He hasn't called me that since the third grade, thought Markham. He raised his head and looked up.

His son leaned over him, struggling to lift him under the arms.

He tried to speak "Where . . . ?"

It was so cold his teeth were chattering. Was the window broken? Eddie must have felt it, too, the way he kept looking outside through the panes that were no longer there. Or was he listening to the animals thrashing in the bushes beside the house?

Somehow Markham managed to stand on his own. "Where are they?"

"Come on, Dad, lie down." Eddie's lips were quivering. "Please . . . !"

He examined his hands and arms under the bright light, felt the front of his shirt. She hadn't cut him. "I'm all right. It's just my—"

My heart, he thought.

Hell of a time for it.

"My pills. I need my pills."

"Where?"

"In the kitchen," he lied. It was necessary to get outside. "Help me . . ."

With the pins-and-needles in his legs he had no choice but to move slowly.

When they got to the kitchen, he saw nothing outside. The night was still except for the big engines in the distance. The fire must have been almost out by now; the horizon was nearly black beyond the fence.

Then he heard a low grunt.

He stumbled around the backpack on the floor and made it to the screen porch.

As his eyes adjusted a large knot of flesh became visible, like a photographic negative developing. He saw a leg kick, heard another grunt. The two women must have crashed through the bedroom window and taken the fight to the backyard. What part of the human knot was Evie?

He flicked on the porch light.

The younger one was on top. Her body was dirty and streaked with scratches, as though she had been dragged out the window and along the side of the house. He saw wood chips and sawdust clinging to her small breasts, which meant that she had to be facing the sky.

Evie was underneath. She had the extension cord from the leaf shredder wrapped around the girl's throat, pulling with white fingers. Her lips were curled back and her teeth were bared.

He had to stop them, but no sound came from his mouth. His throat was dry and his tongue thick as leather.

The girl arched her back and tried to bridge. Evie held her, but now the cord was slipping through her fingers.

CALIFORNIA GOTHIC

He took the porch steps slowly to keep the band from tightening around his chest. One step at a time and he would get there. He moved like the walking dead, but any faster and he would not make it at all.

He managed to pick up the chain saw with his one good hand.

There was no way to yank the cord and get it started. The tank was empty anyway; he had run it down to fumes only hours ago.

Even if he could get it running, what would he do? Cut them apart?

He needed help.

Where was Eddie?

The girl freed herself and reared up, facing him. She no longer had the knife. Only a quizzical, unblinking look. She tilted her head to one side.

"Kill her," she said to him.

He ignored her and dropped down next to Evie. The break in the skin across her stomach was superficial but there were other cuts, and her cheekbones were bleeding. She was having trouble getting up, as if something was wrong with her spine.

He did his best to help her.

It was not enough.

"All right," the girl said, "I'll do it."

She took the chain saw from him and pulled the cord three times. When it would not start she looked around, and saw the gas can next to the garage.

She set the chain saw down and unscrewed the top of the can. Then she left the saw where it was, by the leaf shredder, and came back.

She tipped the can and poured it out over Evie.

Markham reeled under the acrid fumes. He squeezed his eyes closed and reached out blindly for the spout. Evie screamed and screamed as the gasoline splashed into the cuts. The liquid ran through his fingers like hot oil. The fumes filled his lungs and the band around his chest grew tighter.

The girl set her bare foot into his side and kicked, to roll him away.

He got his eyes open again.

Eddie was on the porch. He had the backpack. He reached into it and took out a gun, a heavy .45 automatic. The muzzle wobbled as he pointed it, swinging from the girl to Evie and back again, searching for a target.

"It won't work with the safety on," the girl told him matter-of-factly.

She dropped the can and took a step back, standing clear. The can fell into the hole Markham had dug as her heels came to rest on the edge.

Markham began to crawl toward her, one inch at a time, not taking his eyes off her ankles.

CALIFORNIA GOTHIC

A shove, that's all it would take, and she would topple into darkness . . .

Then she stepped forward, away from the hole, and gazed past Eddie, at the lighted kitchen behind him.

"Do you have a match?" she asked.

"Why are you standing on the porch?"

Her voice was muffled but still clear through the darkness. Markham raised his knees and pushed himself higher, concentrating on the circle of light before him.

"This is a bad time," said the other voice.

"No, it's not. You're family!"

"Yeah, right . . ."

"Well, almost. What is *that*?"

"I thought he could use it. For the bedroom."

"Oh, Lennie, you didn't have to! Come on in . . ."

The plywood walls rattled with the echo of footsteps, and the bedroom door opened.

"Hey, buddy," said Len.

"Hey, yourself." Markham lowered the writing board from the circle of light on his lap and set it aside. "What you got?"

Len entered, carrying a small, bulky shape. "Just my old TV. So you can catch some flicks."

"Thanks, man."

"*Por nada*. Where do you want it?"

She stood behind Len, dimly outlined against the open doorway, considering. Then she came all the way in, bringing with her a little bit of the daylight from the rest of the house. She started clearing off the dresser. "Up here, for now. Where's our old TV stand?"

"In the garage," said Markham. "It's rusty, but it should work."

"I'll get it . . . Lennie, sit down." She patted the end of the bed. "How about lunch? I was going to make something for Dan."

"Thanks, but I can't stay."

She leaned over to plant a kiss on Markham's forehead. "What'll it be, love? Soup or sandwich?"

"Later." Markham tipped his head back and touched his lips to hers. "You go ahead, if you want. I'm not very hungry."

She nodded and stood again, moving away from the swing-arm lamp and back into the semidarkness. Behind her, a long, thin thread of daylight leaked into the room from the covered bedroom window, like a pale lightning bolt that started a few inches above her head, only to be absorbed by her silhouette. She paused, turned impulsively and gave Len a hug.

CALIFORNIA GOTHIC

"What's that for?" Len said.

"Do I have to have a reason?" Then she said to Markham, "If you need me, whistle."

"I will."

"She's looking great," Len said when she was gone. "Like Betty Bacall. *The Big Sleep*."

"*To Have and Have Not*," said Markham. "She *is* great. She took care of everything."

Lenny found the wheelchair folded against the closet door. "Mind if I try this? I never sat in one before."

"Go ahead. Knock yourself out."

Lennie got the sides apart, sat in the wheelchair and rolled it back and forth. "Marlon Brando," he said. "*The Men*."

"And *Bedtime Story*. With David Niven."

"I knew that," said Len, testing the new toy. "You don't really need this, do you?"

"They make you use one when you leave the hospital. Evie wanted to rent it." Markham adjusted the pillow at his back. "Are Katie's parents in town yet?"

"At the Day's Inn. The funeral's set for one tomorrow."

"I'll be there."

"Sure? Jeannie and I are picking them up. We can come by."

"I'm sure. We'll meet you."

Lennie kicked away from the floor and spun

the chair, popping a wheelie. "I like this. *Hell's Angels on Wheels.*"

"Don't go near the window. There might be some glass in the carpet."

"Is that how she got those cuts?"

Markham nodded. "It wasn't bad. She didn't even want to see the doctor."

"Afraid of stitches?"

"I don't think she's afraid of anything, now."

Outside, the sound of children's laughter rang from the elementary school a few blocks away, penetrating the sheet of plywood.

"She put that up herself?" said Len, pointing at the covered window.

"Sure did. Measured it, cut it and nailed it. She wouldn't let me help. I'll get the glazier in here tomorrow."

"It'll cost."

"Yeah, I know. I could do it myself, but she won't let me." Markham propped his writing board against his knees and repositioned the lamp so that it shone directly onto the white bond paper. "It was my fault. A stupid-ass thing. I must have hit the window when I fell."

"You don't remember?"

"Only parts. I was on the floor—I blacked out. I don't know how I got to the front lawn. They say that's where I was, when the ambulance came. Maybe she carried me. She doesn't want to talk about it."

"You're lucky," said Len. "I mean, what's the point? Some shit it's better not to remember, right?"

"Right."

"So. You need anything?"

"I'm not an invalid, Len. It was a myocardial infarct. I just have to take it easy for a while. I can come back to the store anytime."

"I was thinking we should stay closed a few more days."

Markham nodded. Then he said, "Is the gun still there?"

"The .38? Locked in the drawer. You want it?"

"No. Just asking."

Len looked at him curiously. "They'll get her."

"I know they will."

"The Mystery Girl. When she tries to pull something else. They dusted the store for prints, and the book locker. Trying to find a match. Now they'll run them through the computer and see what comes up."

"If they have her prints on file."

"They have prints on everybody. Even if she's never been busted. They're on the birth certificate."

"Maybe she doesn't have a birth certificate."

Len laughed. "You sound like me."

The sunlight grew brighter, more intense around the edges of the plywood, as the California sun rose higher in the sky, angling down mercilessly on the old house.

"Do I?"

"Write it up," said Len, "and send it to *Mother Jones*. 'The Agents of Chaos.' Invisible terrorists in our midst . . ."

"I'll leave that to you." The warning bell rang at the school and Markham started at the sound, jerking his pen involuntarily across the paper. He tried to begin again. "I'm working on something else."

"What?"

"I thought I'd try a poem."

"Yeah?"

"It's been awhile."

"It sure has!" Len grinned.

"I said *try*. It's one I started a long time ago. I wanted to make a few changes. But I can't get it right."

"You will. Just hang in there. I brought you some movies, when you're finished."

"You did?"

"The tape's in the VCR—that combo unit I bought for Jean. I finally got her a better one, but she doesn't watch it, either."

"What movies?"

"Oldies but goodies. Slow speed, but they look okay. You'll see."

"Thanks."

The second lunch bell rang for the playgroup.

CALIFORNIA GOTHIC

This time Markham was ready for it. He held his ballpoint steady and did not flinch.

"Lucky the fire didn't take out the school," said Len.

"They got to it in time. I guess there were engine companies all the way from Northridge."

"Like a war zone. What's the body count?"

"Only one. They think it was the guy who owned the Pick-A-Part."

"Don't they know?"

"He was burned pretty badly. No fingers left."

"Then they can use dental charts."

Markham continued to stare at the paper before him. He clicked the pen against his teeth. "How do they do that, Len?" he asked. "Do you know?"

"I guess they check the records of all the dentists."

"What if there aren't any records?"

"Then they're shit out of luck." Len's face screwed into an ironic smirk. "It could be Jimmy Hoffa. See, they kept his body all these years, and then they set the fire and threw him in. With somebody else's false teeth, of course . . ."

"That's too far out. Even for you."

"Then—I got it. It's the CSR! Maybe that letter *was* real! See, Judy what's-her-name never died. She substituted a body at the last minute, so there'd be somebody else's fingerprints. She escaped, and her friends have been hiding all these years, a bunch of wackos, waiting to get revenge on the system and take what's theirs. What they *think* is theirs. They've been biding their time till the signal . . ."

"What signal?" said Markham, without expression.

"Who the hell knows? It could be anything. A news report, say. When they hear it, they go into action. Pick up right where they left off. Because they know their leader is back! They hit banks, offices, the IRS . . ."

"Except they weren't terrorists. I told you that."

"But they *were* revolutionaries . . ."

"They'd be older now. Too mellow for a revolution."

"Don't stop me," said Len, "I'm on a roll! Now they're completely nuts, right? So—"

"They hit a *warehouse*, Len. Who would do that? Book burglars?"

"The Nazis burned books, didn't they?"

"Give me a break! They burned a *junkyard*?"

"That was a mistake. To cover their tracks. What they were *really* after was somebody at the bookstore. The same person they thought would be at the warehouse later . . ."

"Who? Katie?"

"*You!*"

Markham's face twitched. "Why?"

CALIFORNIA GOTHIC

"I haven't figured that out yet. Maybe you betrayed her . . ."

"But I didn't."

"Then she had some other motive. Some secret obsession . . . Or maybe it wasn't even her."

"Who was it?"

"How the hell do I know? One of her disciples. Her daughter, say, all grown-up now . . ."

"Len—"

"Follow me. First she goes to your house, but you're not here. So she goes to the bookstore—you're not there, either. Katie tells her where you'll be, and somebody *else* goes over to do it. Only you aren't there yet. Katie is. She got in the way . . ."

"You know what, Len?"

"What?" Len was panting with emotion, his face shining.

"You're so full of shit your eyes are brown."

Len forced himself to take several deep breaths. "Yeah. I know." He looked down at the shadows around his feet, at nothing, and said in a lower, more controlled voice, "Seriously? You didn't have a God damned thing to do with it. It was just a fucking gang girl, looking to steal some shit for her boyfriend. But Katie fought back. So she did her right there. For what? No reason. I wish I could give it one, so it means something. But it doesn't. That's why it hurts."

"I know, Len. I know."

"Me, I'm just jacking off. Forget it."

"Done."

Len put his head back and closed his eyes for a moment. Then he got up shakily from the wheelchair. He looked older.

"I gotta go."

"So go," said Markham. "Thanks for coming by. Say good-bye, Lennie."

"Good-bye, Lennie."

"Oh, and Len?"

"Yeah?"

"You were wrong about one thing."

"What?"

"Jack Nicholson made some good pictures in the seventies—*Marvin Gardens* wasn't the last one. Besides *The Passenger*, there was *Cuckoo's Nest*. And *The Last Detail*."

"Okay. I guess. Were we talking about that?"

"The other day. I remember that much."

Len's eyes were twinkling again. "You're right. The seventies were the Golden Age, when you think about it. For movies, anyway."

"Silver, at least. 'Bye."

Len let himself out the front door.

Markham lay there in the bed with his knees up as the VW chugged away, its valves sucking air. Markham blinked and glanced around as if waking up, then repositioned the lamp over his worksheet. In the strong yellow-white light

CALIFORNIA GOTHIC

from the bulb, his hand appeared frail and heavily veined. He studied it with detachment for a few seconds, frowned, picked up his pen again and made a few corrections to the stanzas he had been working on, so that they read:

> *I sing this song of you*
> *Of bones grown wrong and*
> *Eyes turned back to ash*
> *I sing this song of you*
>
> *Face faded now like*
> *A poster made through carbon*
> *Wrists sharp as knives*
> *Angled in upon yourself . . .*

Distracted, he gave up for the moment. He set the lap desk aside and got out of bed.

The TV sat on the chest of drawers across the room. He found the cord and plugged it into the wall. Then he turned the set on and waited for it to crackle to life.

A newscaster's voice came up before there was a picture.

"In Northern California, a second forest fire victim, this time a male, has been identified as Samuel David Carlisle, a four-year veteran of the Forest Service. Dental records on the female . . ."

He watched the screen intently for another

minute. When the news story ended, he found the POWER button on the bottom panel of the set and pressed it. The built-in VCR immediately ejected a cassette. Markham reinserted it and pressed PLAY. Then he went back to the bed again, leaning against the pillow on the headboard.

The soundtrack warbled and the image rolled, then stabilized as the movie began.

He smiled at the familiar title. As the opening credits came into focus, he looked again at his paper.

He turned the page over and on the back of the poem wrote three words in large block letters:

THERE ARE OTHERS

Farther down, he added:

HOW MANY?

Then, at the bottom of the page, he made a further note to himself:

NUMBER OF MEMBERS IN THE CSR

Under that he wrote:

NUMBER OF BODIES FOUND

CALIFORNIA GOTHIC

And under that:

DENTAL RECORDS??

He circled the last sentence, then put the pen down and sat back, staring into space, as a woman's voice spoke to him from the TV set across the dim bedroom.

"I Walked with a Zombie . . . It does seem an odd thing to say. Had anyone said that to me a year ago, I'm not at all sure I would have known what a zombie was! I might have had some notion that they were strange and frightening, even a little funny. It all began in such an ordinary way . . ."

The TV set in the den was on, too, but so far all that could be seen was a storm of grainy particles.

Evie hummed to herself as she stopped off on her way to the kitchen.

"Would you boys like some lunch?"

"Not now, Mom," said Eddie.

"No, thanks, Mrs. Markham," said Tommy. He had his video camera plugged into the back of the TV.

"What are you watching?"

"Oh, just some tape Tommy shot."

"Why don't you put it in the VCR?"

"It's the wrong format," said Eddie.

"Then how are you going to watch it?"

"You can use the camera. It plays back, if you don't have a Hi-8 deck."

"Well, we'll just have to get one, won't we? That's a nice camera . . . How's your mother, Tommy?"

"She's fine."

"And your brother Mike?"

"Okay. He's got a cast on his arm. But they didn't press charges."

"That's the least they can do!" she said. "It was the LAPD's fault. You're lucky you didn't get hurt, too."

"I know."

"Well, you know where the food is," she called from the hall. "Help yourself . . ."

"Mom?"

"Yes?"

"Where are you going?"

"Just outside. I thought I'd water the yard. Pretty soon it will be green again—it's already started. By the end of the summer, it will all be grown over. You won't be able to recognize it."

"Do you need me to help?"

"You've done more than enough, baby—excuse me. Eddie."

When she left, Eddie plugged the patch cord into the video camera and pushed a button. The TV screen rolled, then stabilized into a grainy,

CALIFORNIA GOTHIC

desaturated blur. Only Reggae Rat's head was clearly silhouetted, like a tiki god in an island sunset. The rest of the frame was underexposed.

"Nothing," said Tommy.

"That's all right," said Eddie. "I didn't get anything, anyway. You can erase it."

"Wait, I think I see—"

"You don't see anything. *We* didn't see anything. Okay?"

Tommy watched his friend's face. "Okay."

Eddie shut off the camera.

"You can borrow it, if you want," said Tommy. "I have to finish my term paper. Did you do yours?"

"I haven't started."

"It's due Friday, remember, bud? That's tomorrow."

"I'll make it up later. I'm staying home again. In case my mother needs me."

"You're lucky," said Tommy. "Your dad's cool, and you don't have a big brother . . . and your mom sure is nice now."

"She fixed up my room. She's going to get me a lot of stuff. Anything I want."

"How come?"

"Because I helped her."

"You mean the yard?"

"Somebody had to clean it up," said Eddie with an oddly flat, characterless grin, as if he knew something that he was not ready to tell anyone, not even his best friend, just yet.

Evie connected the nozzle to the hose and turned on the water. She squirted the back of the house, but the ashes that had floated onto the roof were too high; she would have to use the ladder. Then she soaked the plants, even the weeds, so they would grow together in a thick groundcover, hiding the ugly hole. Even with the dirt filled in it was an eyesore and likely to draw attention if anyone came into the backyard. Now, with everything buried, the ivy was free to spread in a dense mat. A few more weeks and it would look like it had been here for years.

She raised the hose and shot a high arcing spray into the still air, and in the mist a rainbow appeared over the yard, as though pointing the way to a pot of gold that no one would ever discover unless they knew where to dig.

She adjusted the nozzle to send a full blast of water into the yard, drenching the mound and seeping into the pores of the earth, breaking down organic matter so that it could be reborn as rich loam. It would nourish new life and rebuild their world here, if they decided not to sell the house, after all.

She heard the front door open.

She put down the hose and went into the house.

CALIFORNIA GOTHIC

In the hallway, she saw that Eddie was in his room now, seated at his desk.

"Where's Tommy?"

At the sound of her voice he slipped some papers hurriedly into a folder.

"He had to go home."

"Oh, that's too bad. I hope he says hello to his mother for me. I guess I could call . . . What are you working on?"

"My column."

"Great. Be sure to let me read it when you're done."

"I will." He swiveled in his chair and looked at her. "What are you doing, Mom?"

She held his eyes. Finally she said, "I'm finishing up in the yard."

He held his neck stiff. "Do you need me?"

"Not now. Pretty soon everything will be the way it used to be."

"Will it?"

The kitten ran from under Eddie's desk and rubbed its scent against her leg. She scooped it up and rewarded it with a kiss.

"My brave little one!" she said. Then she looked at Eddie. "You'll see."

"Okay, Mom. If you say so."

He lowered his head and turned the chair back around.

"I'd better check on your father," she said, carrying the kitten away.

DENNIS ETCHISON

* * *

He sat there until he heard their voices in the front bedroom.

Then he opened the folder again.

There were two sheets of twenty-pound bond inside, folded and refolded so many times they were ready to tear. The envelopes, postmarked before he was born, had no return address. They had been mailed to someone named Judy Rios.

One sheet was a typed letter, unsigned. It was written in an elliptical style but seemed to be a recounting of the details and events of one ordinary day, as if the very banality of the descriptions might convey some deeper meaning when set to paper. It was not exactly a love letter, but it was clear that the two people knew each other very well, perhaps intimately. The language was direct enough but the content elusive, as though the real point was not to be found in the words but in the spaces between them, in what was not said.

The other sheet, also typed, contained a poem. The last part of it read:

> *My fingers reach your shoulders*
> *They are moth wings in this light*
> *Your skin stretched to powder*
> *Comes away beneath my touch*

CALIFORNIA GOTHIC

Yet I sing this song of you
Of lips still cool and sweet
As the fruit of desert flowers
I sing this song of you

Who will kiss in sleep
The breathing ache
Of this our strange
Returning

The poem, too, was unsigned.

When he had finished reading it, he sat there and waited to hear the sound of the door to the main bedroom clicking shut.

Then he got up and fished behind his bed, where a backpack was hidden. He took it out, replaced the letter and poem and started to reclose the top flap. He hesitated, took out a Grateful Dead T-shirt, lifted it to his face and breathed deeply. Then he stuffed it back down and returned the backpack to its hiding place.

He sat down at his desk again and opened the top drawer.

Inside was a .45 automatic pistol.

He removed the clip, checked to see that it was indeed full again and did not need to be reloaded with any of the loose shells in the drawer, and then painstakingly, methodically wiped off any fingerprints, using the tail of his shirt. He set it back in exactly the same position, as if repeating a frequent ritual, and closed and locked the drawer.

He left his room.

He went to the den for the video camera, disconnected it and carried it to the back porch, lost in thought. The washer and dryer were running, as they had all morning and most of the week, one load after another, or perhaps the same load over and over. The air was uncomfortably moist and warm. He turned to the screen door and looked out over the yard.

The mound was flowing with water from the hose, clods of fresh, hardpacked dirt breaking away and running off in rivulets of mud.

He went out to turn off the faucet.

Then he sat down on the porch and stared at the mound, studying it. He raised the camera and sighted through the viewfinder.

EXT. DAY - GRAVESITE

MOVING IN on a rectangle of dirt. No grass grows anywhere near this particular plot . . .

Now a YOUNG MAN—EDWARD, early teens but mature, handsome—approaches the grave warily. He has the look of a young poet about him, sensitive and tortured.

CALIFORNIA GOTHIC

He kneels and plucks a moist clod from the grave. His hand closes tightly as he is wracked with emotion. The dirt squeezes out between his fingers.

>EDWARD
>(weeping)
>Why . . . why . . . ?

WIDER—to show a *headstone* behind the grave.

MOVING IN on the lettering, almost all of which is covered with dirt, except for the first letter of the first name:

>"S"

And beneath that:

>*"Rest in Peace"*

The dates of her birth and death are obscured.

He pounds his fist against the granite.

>EDWARD
>Sorry . . . I'm sorry . . .
>I didn't know who you were,

**and now it's too late!
I never knew you at all . . . !**

Now the dirt on the mound begins to swell and expand—as if something buried there is attempting to rise up and burst through to this world . . .

Suddenly a *knife blade* thrusts up into the air—

And *impales him*—passing through his Adam's apple—and out the back of his neck!

He lowered the camera.
The dirt had not moved. The mound was unchanged.
He sat with the camera in his lap, a tense but resigned expression on his face. As the afternoon wore on, it began to appear that he might sit there for a very long time, even past sundown and into the night, if necessary, waiting for a sign.

DISCOVER THE TRUE MEANING OF HORROR...

Poppy Z. Brite

- ☐ LOST SOULS .... 21281-2 .... $4.99
- ☐ DRAWING BLOOD .... 21492-0 .... $4.99

Kathe Koja

- ☐ THE CIPHER .... 20782-7 .... $4.99
- ☐ BAD BRAINS .... 21114-X $4.99
- ☐ SKIN .... 21115-8 .... $4.99

Tanith Lee

- ☐ DARK DANCE .... 21274-X $4.99
- ☐ HEART-BEAST .... 21455-6 .... $4.99
- ☐ PERSONAL DARKNESS .... 21470-X $4.99

Melanie Tem

- ☐ PRODIGAL .... 20815-7 .... $4.50
- ☐ WILDING .... 21285-5 .... $4.99
- ☐ MAKING LOVE .... 21469-6 .... $4.99
   (co-author with Nancy Holder)
- ☐ REVENANT .... 21503-X $4.99

- ☐ GRAVE MARKINGS/Michael Arnzen ..... 21339-8 .... $4.99
- ☐ X,Y/Michael Blumlein .... 21374-6 .... $4.99
- ☐ DEADWEIGHT/Robert Devereaux .... 21482-3 .... $4.99
- ☐ SHADOWMAN/Dennis Etchison .... 21202-2 .... $4.99
- ☐ HARROWGATE/Daniel Gower .... 21456-4 .... $4.99
- ☐ DEAD IN THE WATER/Nancy Holder .... 21481-5 .... $4.99
- ☐ 65MM/Dale Hoover .... 21338-X $4.99

At your local bookstore or use this handy page for ordering:

DELL READERS SERVICE, DEPT. DS
2451 South Wolf Road, Des Plaines, IL 60018

Please send me the above title(s). I am enclosing $ _____ .
(Please add $2.50 per order to cover shipping and handling). Send check or money order—no cash or C.O.D.s please.

Ms./Mrs./Mr. _____

Address _____

City/State _____ Zip _____

DAB–11/94

Prices and availability subject to change without notice. Please allow four to six weeks for delivery.

SCIENCE FICTION/FANTASY

☐ **CHUNG KUO: THE MIDDLE KINGDOM** (SF)   20761-4 $5.99/$7.50 Can.
By David Wingrove.

☐ **CHUNG KUO II: THE BROKEN WHEEL** (SF)   20928-5 $5.99/$6.99 Can.
By David Wingrove.

☐ **CHUNG KUO III: THE WHITE MOUNTAIN** (SF)   21356-8 $5.99/$6.99 Can.
By David Wingrove.

☐ **MASKS OF THE ILLUMINATI**   50306-X $9.95/$12.95 Can.
By Robert Anton Wilson.
A LARGE FORMAT PAPERBACK.

☐ **THE ILLUMINATUS! TRILOGY**   53981-1 $14.95/$17.95 Can.
By Robert J. Shea & Robert Anton Wilson.
A LARGE FORMAT PAPERBACK.

☐ **SCHRODINGER'S CAT TRILOGY**   50070-2 $13.95/$16.95 Can.
By Robert Anton Wilson.
A LARGE FORMAT PAPERBACK.

☐ **CHUNG KUO: THE STONE WITHIN** (SF)   50569-0 $14.95/$17.95 Can.
By David Wingrove.
A LARGE FORMAT PAPERBACK.

At your local bookstore or use this handy page for ordering:
DELL READERS SERVICE, DEPT. DFS
2451 South Wolf Road, Des Plaines, IL 60018

Please send me the above title(s). I am enclosing $ _____
(Please add $2.50 per order to cover shipping and handling). Send check or money order—no cash or C.O.D.s please.

Ms./Mrs./Mr. _____

Address _____

City/State _____ Zip _____

DFS–6/95

Prices and availability subject to change without notice. Please allow four to six weeks for delivery.